Mabel Osgood Wright

Tommy-Anne and the three hearts

Mabel Osgood Wright

Tommy-Anne and the three hearts

ISBN/EAN: 9783337123796

Printed in Europe, USA, Canada, Australia, Japan

Cover: Foto ©Andreas Hilbeck / pixelio.de

More available books at **www.hansebooks.com**

TOMMY-ANNE

AND

THE THREE HEARTS

The lives and habits of plants and animals, however fancifully treated in this book, are in strict accordance with the known facts of their existence.

Tommy-Anne stood in the doorway tying a knot in the elastic of her hat. — p. 2.

TOMMY-ANNE

AND

THE THREE HEARTS

BY

MABEL OSGOOD WRIGHT

AUTHOR OF "BIRDCRAFT," "THE FRIENDSHIP OF NATURE," ETC.

WITH ILLUSTRATIONS

BY ALBERT D. BLASHFIELD

New York

THE MACMILLAN COMPANY

LONDON: MACMILLAN & CO., LTD.

1897

Norwood Press
J. S. Cushing & Co. — Berwick & Smith
Norwood Mass. U.S.A.

This Book is Dedicated

TO

MY MOTHER

PREFACE TO THIRD EDITION

TOMMY-ANNE and Waddles went out of doors to find Reason Why, and I have tried to tell you how they found him.

The winds whispered to Tommy-Anne, and the birds sung to her; she knew that they bore messages, but she could not understand them until Heart of Nature came to help her.

Reason Why is always roving about the fields and woods, often creeping indoors, or sunning himself in winter in a warm garden corner. Go out and question him for yourselves, you healthy, happy children. If the weather is very cold, coax him in by the fireside. You will find that the Three Hearts are always ready to interpret for you, for the thing that they love best is the pure child-heart, whether its owner is seven or seventy.

M. O. W.

WALDSTEIN, FAIRFIELD, CT.,
 Christmas Day, 1896.

CONTENTS

LIST OF ILLUSTRATIONS

INDIAN WORDS

(Chiefly Algonkian)

Adjidau'mo . . . . The Red Squirrel.
A'moe . . . . The Honey Bee.
Bukada'win . . . . Famine.
Chetowaik . . . . The Plover.
Dahin'da . . . . The Bull Frog.
Ghee'zis . . . . The Sun.
Gitche-ah-mo . . . . The Bumble Bee.
Gushkewau' . . . . The Darkness.
Kabibonok'ka . . . . The North Wind.
Keeway'din . . . . The North West Wind.
Ko'ko'ko'ho . . . . The Horned Owl.
Little Oo-oo . . . . The Screech Owl.
Mahng . . . . The Loon.
Ma'ma . . . . The Woodpecker.
Miskodeed . . . . The Spring Beauty.
Moon of Leaves . . . . May.
Moon of Strawberries . . . June.
Moon of Falling Leaves . . . September.
Moon of Snow-Shoes . . . November.
Mudjekee'wis . . . . . . The West Wind.
Ondaig . . . . The Crow.
O-o-chug . . . . The Fly.
Ope'chee . . . . The Robin.
Owais'sa . . . . . . The Bluebird.

xv

Pau'guk . . . . Death.
Pe'boan . . . . Winter.
Puk-Wudj'ies . . . . Wild Men. Little van-
                                     ishing people.
Segwun . . . . Spring.
Shawonda'see . . . . The South Wind.
Shaw'shaw . . . . The Swallow.
Shi'sheeb . . . . The Duck.
Subbeka'she . . . . The Spider.
Sugge'ma . . . . The Mosquito.
Tchin-dees . . . . The Jay.
To'tem . . . . Coat of Arms.
Wabas'so . . . . The Rabbit. The Spirit
                                     of the North.
Wa'bun . . . . The East Wind.
Wa'bun An'nung . . . . The Morning Star.
Wabe'no . . . . The Magician.
Wa'wa . . . . The Wild Goose.
Waw'be'ko'ko . . . . The Snow Owl.
Wawonais'sa . . . . The Whip-poor-will.
Weeng . . . . The Spirit of Sleep.

I

THE MAGIC SPECTACLES

IT was so bright out of doors that particular May morning that the house seemed very dark and lonely by comparison. But then, to be sure, Tommy-Anne never liked to stay indoors, and everything was beckoning and calling; so many strange birds winging over the garden, so many strange shapes slipping through the grass. The wind blowing from the hill called: "Come out, if you wish to see things grow!" whispering to the woods as it hurried through: "Make haste, old Oaks, unfurl your flags; summer will soon be here."

Tommy-Anne was not, as might be supposed, a pair of twins, but a little girl with no brothers or sisters. Her real name was Diana, which had been shortened to Anne. Then, as she could climb trees, preferred boys' games to dolls, and asked a great many questions about how things are made, her father called her Tommy-Anne in fun, and the name suited her so well that people very soon forgot that she had any other.

Playing alone in the woods and garden, and doing her lessons seated on the big dictionary close by her father, as he worked in his study, Tommy-Anne had time to think of a great many *whys* and *whats* and *becauses* that very few people understood, and that no one seemed to have time to answer. Her Aunt Prue, who considered Tommy-Anne as odd as her name, and was the only one of the family at home that day, told the child to "go out and try to be like other people," simply because she had asked a few particularly difficult *whys*.

Tommy-Anne stood in the doorway, tying a knot in the elastic of her hat, and wondering why *her* hat would not stick on without being fastened, as the butcher-boy's did.

Two odours perplexed her inquisitive nose, — cake in process of baking and a breath of the first apple blossoms. Without hesitating, she started in the direction of the orchard; but her little rabbit-hound, Waddles, was more interested in the cake. He raised his pointed muzzle in the air, sniffed, then gave a short bay and looked at his mistress appealingly.

"No, it's not a bit of use, Waddles, wishing for things out of time, when Aunt Prue is at home alone. Aunt Prue says things must be as they are ordered. Now, that's all very well for things that one can't help, but *why* do people make unnecessary rules and say they must be kept just because they've been made? Cake is for supper and pudding for dinner, Waddles! Never cake *before* dinner, and it's only after breakfast now. Did you ever have cake *before* dinner?" Whereupon Waddles looked very knowing, and gave a few short barks to signify that he believed that he had.

"I suspect that you are a glutton, Mr. Waddles," Tommy-Anne continued. "Come, let's run up-hill, for you certainly are too fat and need exercise. Doesn't the air make you want to curl up your feet and make wings of your ears, and fly? What a lovely bat you would make, Waddlekins! Twenty times as big as Dusky Wings, that comes out of the attic window every night." And Tommy-Anne spread her arms and rushed up the slope, the hound following her in full cry.

She dropped at the foot of the first tree that she reached, which happened to be an old white oak, and, after she stopped panting, pulled a handful of willow whistles, that the butcher-boy had made, from her pocket, and began sorting them into her lap. She blew each one in turn, but was dissatisfied with them all. "If I only understood the birds' language, then they would answer me," she said.

"Bob-white! Bob-white!" called a quail from the brush lot.

"Ah! that is plain enough; he is telling me his name. I can talk to *him*."

"Bob-white!" she blew clearly on her longest whistle. For several minutes Tommy-Anne and the quail exchanged greetings, and then he changed his note to — "*Poor Bob-white.*"

"Poor Bob-white" — she answered readily. "He must be trying to tell me about his unfortunate relations who were killed by the gunners last fall. No, that can't be it either; I'm all boggled up. He is talking *my* language, but I'm not learning *his* a bit," and she stretched herself on the moss, her chin on her hands.

"I wish I knew *why*," sighed Tommy-Anne, looking up through the branches.

" Why what ? " said a Voice close beside her.

" Why everything," she replied, looking about, expecting to see the owner of the voice.

The house stood quite below her, the garden and orchard coming between. In the other direction trees, in sociable groups of twos and threes, straggled along until they crowded together to make the wood at the top of the hill. It was very still for a moment; she could hear the river bubbling over the stones beyond the highway, the horse stamping as he shifted his footing in the stable.

" This is very queer," said Tommy-Anne, addressing Waddles, who was lying at her feet. " Didn't you hear some one speak ? Why don't you bark, sir ? "

She walked around the oak and toward the wood, but finding no one, returned to her seat, and leaning her back against the tree, said more earnestly than before, " I *do* wish I knew *why*."

" WHY WHAT ? " said the Voice, very much louder than before.

Tommy-Anne jumped to her feet and looked at the great Oak, for the Voice came from that direction. All that could be seen was the furrowed trunk, whose bark was split and scarred by weather and decay. She put her ear to a little crack and listened.

"Yes, I am here," said the Voice; "I was here before. Why is it that when you House People look for a clue, you search the corners of the earth for what is close at home? We Wood Folk know that as a trail ends in cover it cannot begin in the open."

"Really, really I don't know," said Tommy-Anne, in confusion. "I never heard a tree talk before, and I was looking for a *person*, you see."

"I am not a tree," said the Voice, "though I seem to be living in one now."

"Oh, I am so glad," she cried. "Because if you are clever enough to get into a tree, perhaps you can tell me some *whys*.

"I should be very glad to help you to get out. Please, how shall I begin? Shall I scoop a hole in the tree with my knife? It's a rather slow knife, though."

The Voice did not answer for several minutes, and then it sounded directly in her ear.

"What are the things you want to know, Tommy-Anne?" it said.

"All the *whys* and *whats* and *becauses*, the reasons for things," she answered eagerly. "But how did you know my name when I don't know yours?"

She put her ear to a little crack and listened. —p. 6.

" That is easily told," said the Voice ; " I have often heard your father calling you."

" Of course ! how stupid of me! I might have known that, for if it had been Aunt Prue that you heard, she would have said Di-a-n-a, and you would never have guessed that my usual name is Tommy-Anne.

" I want to know so many things," she continued. " Everything about the garden and the woods, the water and the sky. If the flowers are sorry that they can't move about, and what they think of ; where the birds spend the winter, and why they sing before they go to sleep. I want to know what all the noises are, that I hear in the woods when it is dark ; why the rain does not put the fireflies' lights out, and where the butterflies come from. Then there is the river, too ; it always says the same thing when it tumbles over the dead willow below the bridge ; it seems as if I *must* understand it."

" If you wish to know so many things, Tommy-Anne," said the Voice, " you must go to Whyland and see for yourself, for there everything tells its own story, and each one sees and hears what he most desires."

> " Whyland, thy land,
> Away in the cannibal island ! "

she repeated. "The Butcher-boy knows a song that goes something like that, only I am not very sure of the words. Is it near Wonderland, where Alice met the mad March Hare and the Cheshire Cat? Or by Fairyland, where Riquet with the Tuft and the Sleeping Beauty lived? Perhaps it is the North Country, where the Storks build their nests on the chimney stones, and the poor little Tin Soldier floated down the gutter, and the Street Lamp was so sad?"

"No, Tommy-Anne; the people in Whyland are real people, though their speech is so strange to the House People that they think it fairy talk. Whyland covers the whole earth; and though I am a ruler in it, yet there are different interpreters to teach its languages, for no one may learn them all.

"You are a thoughtful child (the heedless can never learn even one of these languages), so you may learn the speech of the nearest corner and the ways of its people, and see them through the Magic Spectacles, that give both sight and hearing to those who wear them."

"Magic Spectacles?"

"Yes, surely; for no one can more than *peep* into Whyland without them, and then it seems a dreary place — all facts and figures like the multiplication table.

"In Whyland the talk I would teach you is of the NEARBY! The speech of the small river ; of the Fox that drinks of it ; of the Water Snake that spreads its dark folds on the overhanging grape-vine ; of the Red Squirrel in the corn-crib ; of the Mole tunnelling the garden path ; of the Woodchuck slinking through the field ; of the Coon in his tree hollow ; and the Wild Cat that creeps to the wood edge at the first snow-fall.

"The talk of the feathered brothers as they follow the year around, from the first Bluebird to the great Snowy Owl that comes when the Christmas trees are trimmed.

"You shall learn the language of the flowers that you tie for a bouquet, of the ferns that live in the deep woods, and are so shy that they speak only to the mosses ; you shall hear the tales that the old trees tell, as they rock to and fro croon-ing. The brotherhood that I may teach you of, is of the Beehive and The Little Beasts Near Home."

"What must I take with me to Whyland, dear Tree Man?" asked Tommy-Anne.

"You need not carry anything but your mind ; for without that you cannot see even through the Magic Spectacles."

"Oh! I know one *what* already," she cried, clapping her hands after a little habit of her own, because very often when she was glad she had no one to tell it to; "I know what *absent-minded* means, now. It is not to see what is straight under your nose, because your *thinker* is somewhere else! Dear Mr. Tree Man, please, please, tell me your real name and what the Magic Spectacles are made of, and how long I may wear them. I thought that magic things were not really-trulies."

"The House People have a habit of calling many things that they cannot understand with their every-day eyes, magical or untrue, but I cannot tell you how the Magic Spectacles are made until you have worn them. While you have them on *you* will understand the speech of beasts and birds, while *they* will not fear you; and you shall wear these spectacles until Christmas eve.

"Remember! the pass-word in this new world is Brotherhood!"

A breeze blew Tommy-Anne's hair about her face, and as she shook it back and tucked the curly ends under the ribbon, everything appeared to be more distinct, and she heard a babel of soft voices.

"The Magic Spectacles! I have the Magic Spectacles, though I can't feel them," she cried, putting her hands to her eyes. Looking up, she saw an old man standing where the Oak tree had been. At least, she thought at the first glance that he was old, because everything about him seemed gray; when she looked again, she saw that it was not the gray of age, but rather the colour of the pearly mist that follows the spring rains and makes the earth bud forth. His face was kindly, though many varying expressions passed over it, some tender, some very stern. Tommy-Anne was puzzled; it was unlike any face that she had ever seen before.

"Are you very old, Tree Man?" she asked timidly.

"I have lived a great many years, if that is what you mean by being old. But if you understand age as nearing the end of life as you know it, then I am young."

"Your name; please tell me your real name before you go," begged Tommy-Anne, as she saw that the form of the Tree Man was melting away in the branches of the Oak.

Pausing a moment, he said: "Listen child; there are Three Hearts that together rule everything, the *seen* and the *unseen*: each has a law and language of its own, which you will learn in time. I am one of these rulers, though not the greatest, and my name is — Heart of Nature."

Then the great Oak stood alone, and through all the treetops there ran a mysterious whisper: "Heart o' Nature! Heart o' Nature!"

"We are in great luck, aren't we, Waddles?" said Tommy-Anne, after a long silence. "I do not think I understand exactly what the Tree Man means about the Three Hearts, but I suppose he will tell me before next Christmas. Oh, Waddles dear! when we can ask as many questions as we please and have them answered, *don't* you think it will be very hard to have to go into the house at night?"

"The Tree Man did not say that you must not ask questions in the house."

"No; I don't remember that he did; but I hardly think it would be polite in us to trouble the beasts and things to come so far from home; and suppose Aunt Prue was to see them! Of course we can talk to the mice, and there are sometimes nice big ants in the sugar-jar, but we had better save those for rainy days."

"I do not mind staying out all night, if it's moonlight, but I do hope you will not forget dinner time; you often do now," said the hound, with a sigh.

"Why! how plainly you can answer me," cried Tommy-Anne, in delight; "I never understood more than half that you used to say."

"No, mistress, you did *not*," said Waddles, complacently. "You never *would* understand, though I kept saying the same thing over and over again. I always had to push and jump, make faces or wag my tail, before you would attend to me. That is the reason why I sometimes helped myself, to save you trouble; but your aunt always mistakes my motives and cuffs my ears.

"By the way, now that we understand each other, would you mind telling your aunt *never* to cuff my ears? You cannot tell how it upsets my brain and makes it roar until tears come in my eyes, and all day long I can hardly tell a rat from a rabbit, and then you scold me and call me dumpish. An ache in ears like mine is ten times as big as it is in little ones like yours. Yet, when you have an earache you go to bed and have a nice, soft, hot-water bag to comfort it, while most likely *I* end the day in the wood-house." And Waddles looked up at Tommy-Anne with a very sad expression in his great brown eyes.

"Oh, doggie!" she cried, standing him up on his hind legs and squeezing his cold nose against her cheek, while she drew his silky ears gently through her hand. "I've pulled you about by these often, but I'll never do it again; I'm *so* sorry." Whereupon Waddles gave her a forgiving little kiss, which, according to the best dog etiquette, was a dainty lick on the end of her nose.

As Tommy-Anne stooped over him, she heard a faint sound coming from the ground. Pressing her ear to the sod, she laid her finger on her lips, whispering, "Hush, Waddles! Down close! I can hear the grass grow!"

II

HOW THE GRASS GREW

"Push, thrust! Push, thrust! Now all together!" whispered the small voices.

"Jump up, Waddles, quick!" cried Tommy-Anne. "See what you've been sitting on." Waddles raised himself slowly from force of habit, for his mistress seldom stayed long in one place, and gave a sly smile as if he knew perfectly well that he was sitting on grass, if she did not.

"Pray do not disturb yourselves; I am quite used to being crushed; I rather like it," said a little voice, which Tommy-Anne found proceeded from a blade of grass. "I have some visitors here, however, from the Oak, Beech, and Fir families that feel quite differently."

Looking at what seemed to be merely a stretch of rather dead sod, to which the colour of spring was coming very slowly, Tommy-Anne saw innumerable little spikes like green bayonets, pricking through the brown mat, and as they came up, they called encouragingly to each other. Here and there, between this young grass, appeared the sprouts of stronger plants, some bearing a pair of long, saw-edged leaves pressed together, like hands, palm to palm; others shooting out a half-dozen green spokes at the top of the stem, like a wheel that lacked the tire.

Made bold by the humble manner of the grass, Tommy-Anne asked, "Why are you so late in coming up? The grass in the garden and pasture was green long ago, and down by the river it has been bright all winter."

"For two reasons," said the nearest Grass-blade, shivering a little as it straightened its bayonet. "We are all new here, fresh from the seed, and we are late because the sun forgot to call us."

"Why did the old grass die? It was thick and strong last summer and grew all in little bunches. Waddles and I used often to sit upon it. Do you think that it was discouraged?"

"No, not that; but in this place last Moon of Snow-Shoes, Kabibonokka and Shawondasee fought their great battle, and where they fight the grass is blasted, the bushes shrivel, and even the great oaks themselves bud forth but grudgingly."

"Who are Kabibonokka and Shawondasee, and what is the Moon of Snow-Shoes?" asked Tommy-Anne, with deep interest.

"Pardon me," said the Grass-blade, politely; "I forgot that in our language we still have some names and words that the House People do not use. We learned them from the Red Brothers, the first men who lived with us here, and they understood our secrets, speaking our speech until our language mixed itself with theirs and theirs with ours, and we remember a word from this tribe, another from that. Moon of Snow-Shoes means November, and was in those days the beginning of the season you call winter. Then the deep snows coming early cover everything, so that none could go abroad unless on snow shoes, whose wide, flat, latticed soles slid safely on the crust, and in this way the Red Brothers followed the Fox and Rabbit trails in — "

Here Waddles raised his head, uttered a series of bays that could be heard for miles, circling about the great Oak, head down, as if he was mad; then threw himself on the grass, rolling and whining petulantly.

“ I was very thoughtless,” sighed the Grass-blade, contritely, “ to mention snow and Rabbits before a Rabbit hound ; no wonder it was too much for his feelings. But where were we ? ”

“ You were explaining about the things that fought and killed the grass.”

“ Oh yes! Kabibonokka is the North Wind, and Shawondasee, his rival, the South Wind. The South Wind always has Gheezis, the Sun, for his companion, while the North Wind keeps with him Gushkewau, the short dark days, Wabasso, the Snow Rabbit, the spirit of the North ; while following them, trampling down the Wood Folk, often stalk Bukadawin, Famine, and Pauguk, Death.

“ All plants have blood in them the same as the House People and other animals, only plant blood is very seldom red, but pale and greenish, and you call it sap. In the Moon of Falling Leaves, which is the first month of your autumn, Kabi-

bonokka begins to murmur afar off, and the tree
blood, hearing the sound, creeps from the branches
to the trunk, and from the trunk down to the roots
beneath the ground, to stay there lest it should
freeze while Kabibonokka reigns.

" Then the leaves, having no blood to fill their
veins and nourish them, drop off and dry away.
So Kabibonokka, coming, cries out, 'See how
Shawondasee fears me. All the leaves that sang
to him have fallen before me, trembling; all the
flowers that he wreathed about him are pale and
dead with fear. Even his mate, the sun god
Gheezis, hastens away and leaves short days to
harbour Bukadawin and Pauguk.

" 'Come back, soft Summer Wind, with tender
muscles. Come back, thou, pink-lipped with
strawberry-eating. I, even I, the North Wind,
will wrestle with you for your strengthening!'

" Now the plant blood should stay beneath the
ground, until Heart of Nature calls the South
Wind back, and bids the Sun shine through the
earth and say, 'Up! up! flow up, green sap, and
swell the buds to make the Moon of Leaves,'—
your spring.

" But sometimes Shawondasee is lingering too
near, and hears Kabibonokka's challenge, and
breaking the law, comes back to fight, and then

this evil happens, for evil always follows the breach of Nature's laws.

"Listen! The North Wind whistles, the sap runs down; the South Wind calls, the sap starts to flow upward, thinking its sleep is over. Then upward, downward, while the battle lasts, it goes, until finally, Kabibonokka, satisfied, takes the Snow Owl on his shoulder, and leads Peboan, the Winter, to the northland.

"Then Shawondasee calls again, this time in earnest; but the poor sap, weak and tired (and in the small plants spent and lifeless), answers him slowly, even in the sturdy trees crawling but feebly, not having force to reach the topmost branches, finding in its course many buds, both dead and dying. Then the House People say, 'Look at that treetop; it is winter-killed!' And when this happens, all the hope of life for tender things is in the seed.

"When Heart of Nature is obeyed, then all goes rightly. Kabibonokka and Peboan come together bringing the White Owls with them, and the snow falls thick and covers everything so deeply that the South Wind flies before it, and the tree blood, hearing no disputing, waits in peace."

"Dear Mr. Grass," said Tommy-Anne, "how

could a tiny seed such as you come from, live through this great fight? I helped my father sow some of you last fall, down in the new meadow, and you were like specks of dust."

"Yes; we are only dust-motes borne by the breeze. We were of the seed you scattered, and the wind swept us here under this Oak."

"But," persisted she, "why didn't you grow *then* like the other seeds? why did you wait so long?"

"Because, little House Child, the first lesson we bits of plant life have to learn is — when and how to wait.

"We cannot move from place to place and shift our homes like the animals, according to the seasons and the weather; so from first to last, waiting is our portion.

"The little seed, lying on the ground, waits for the rain and sun to touch it before it may swell and grow; the plant waits for the roots to suck nourishment from the earth and air before it can form the flower; the flower, spreading glowing colours to the sun, or wafting perfume through the night, waits for the Bee, the Butterfly, the Hummingbird, the Moth, to bring it food to fill the little seed germs that it holds within its heart. And, last of all, the bursting pod waits for the wind, the birds, the hand of man, to scatter the seeds afar, lest, falling too close about the parent plant, they choke for lack of soil.

"Back in the Moon of Falling Leaves, when we were blown here to this barren spot, if we had sprouted like our brothers in the warm sheltered meadow, the first rain, gullying down the slope, would have washed us out before we had firm footing. The Voice said *wait* uutil the sun looks backward toward the west at evening and shines full on you from between the birches. For many weeks the clouds hung low, but yesterday the sun remembered us at last, and to-day you see that we are here."

"Who do you mean by the Voice? Was it the Tree Man who gave me the Magic Spectacles?"

"Yes, the very same,— Heart of Nature."

"What do you think of this, Waddles dear, or did you know all about it before?" said Tommy-Anne.

"No, Mistress, I never bothered the grass with such questions ; we always talk upon a different subject. I put my nose down close and whisper, 'What beast tracked through here last, and which way did he run?' The grass always answers me truly — 'this way or that.' If I do not tree the cat or find the rabbit burrow, it is sure to be because you call me back.

"The Tree Man told you that in Whyland each one heard what he wished to hear the most, so you hear the grass say a great many *whys*, but I hear *Cats* and *Rabbits*."

"Get up, you lazy Waddles, and see if we can find the little trees that do not like to be trodden on. Yes, here is one, I am sure ; only you have broken it almost off. I wonder what it would have grown to be."

"An Oak tree," said a vigorous little voice ; "a white Oak like the big one overhead."

Tommy-Anne, looking intently, saw many tender, pinkish green sprouts coming from the ground, each with a few long, wave-edged leaves along its stems. One of them was stretching his leaves and talking.

"Tell me," she asked, "how did you grow so much quicker than the grass? You look very strong and juicy."

"With pleasure, Tommy-Anne," it replied. "Pull up the broken sprout, and I will endeavour to explain."

She drew herself together quite unconsciously, and pulling up the broken tree, held it in her

hand.   The Oak's voice was pleasant, but it
spoke with authority, not humbly like the grass.
For an Oak, no matter how small, never forgets
its dignity, never whispers like a Birch, or titters
and flutters like an Aspen.

" What have you in your hand ? " it continued.

" An acorn, with a crack in it, and a
sprout growing up with leaves on it,
and a sprout growing down with little
hairs on it," she replied ; for she had
been taught by her father to see and
answer accurately ; " but please don't
ask me *whys* and *becauses*, for I don't
know anything, — no, not one thing."

" People who *ask* so many *whys*
and *whats* must answer sometimes to
show that they understand ; and if you
understand *me* you will know how all
trees grow," said the Oak, proudly.

" I was a little speck of oak life,
shut up in an acorn like the one you have in
your hand.   In it I fell to the ground last
season, before the leaves.   About me in the
acorn was packed nice sweet food, to nourish
me in growing until my roots could feed me from
the earth.

" A while ago the Voice called, and at the

sound my heart swelled so with gladness that I burst the shell. The sun called one way, and the moist earth the other; so I reached upward with a hand and groped downward with a foot, though still anchored by the acorn. The sun warmed me, but as yet I could not feed myself, and lived upon the food wrapped up for me, until to-day. Look! now I have a rooting in the soil, and leaves to catch the dew, and I have eaten every bit of my food — the acorn-shell is empty! So is it with all seeds. Of all the plants that creep or climb or float upon the water, great or small, tree or bush, the seed birth is the same."

Tommy-Anne sat still for a long time, her face between her hands; in fact, she was so still that Waddles became nervous and poked his nose into her face anxiously, saying: "Why don't you speak to something else, mistress? This Oak is very gloomy and not over-polite. I should think, after saying so much about food, the least thing it could do would be to offer us something to eat."

"Be still, Waddles; what if it should hear you? Don't you know that Aunt Prue says it is *awful* to ask for anything to eat if you are visiting, even if you are shrivelling with hunger. The most you may *hint* at even is a glass of water."

“ Who is visiting, mistress — we or the Oak ? ” persisted Waddles, sturdily. “ It is *our* ground, you know.”

“ Then the Oaks must be our guests, and we must be very nice to them.”

“ I don’t see why; we did not invite them to come.”

“ For shame, Waddles ! Aren’t you enough of a gentleman to know that you must be extra polite to the people you didn’t invite, so that they will feel comfortable, and not know that there is not *quite* enough for dinner until they get to the table ? ”

“ I don’t see what all that has to do with the — ”

“ Tommy-Anne,” interrupted the Oak, “if that small dog of yours *thinks* he is hungry again, there is Adjidaumo, the Red Squirrel, that lives in the big Oak, whom he might *try* to catch for amusement; and if he is *really* hungry, why doesn’t he dig up the ham bone he buried in the orchard this morning? It was a fine bone, with good meat upon it. The Blacksmith’s cat, Tiger, is smelling around the spot now.”

Up jumped Waddles, his tail standing out like a pump handle, and casting a reproachful look at the tell-tale tree, and a shamefaced one at his mistress, he shot down the hill.

"Then Waddles really did steal that ham, as Aunt Prue said," mused Tommy-Anne to herself. "Never mind; it will take him some time to chase the cat, and I can talk a little longer with the Oak. I don't think it was offended." So she said, "Will you please tell me where the flowers get the food that they pack in the seeds' lunch baskets?"

"That is not for me to explain, child. That story belongs to the messengers of Flowerland, the Hummingbird and the Moon Moth. They will tell it to you when they guide you through the Flower Market and to the Land of Nod."

"The Flower Market and the Land of Nod! Oh, where are they? Are they places in Whyland?"

"Yes; they are in Whyland; the Flower Market is where the Flowers live, from spring to leaf-fall. The Land of Nod is where the Flowers close their eyes and go to sleep.

"If you wish to go to the Flower Market, wait

early in the morning by the tulips in the garden, and when a Hummingbird comes by, wearing a patch of sparkling rubies on his throat, gather a bunch of single tulips and offer them to him, saying, 'Will you breakfast on my flowers, and take me with you to the Flower Market?'

"If he feeds upon the tulips, then you may follow him.

"But if you wish to visit the Land of Nod, then stand at sunset on the garden's border, and presently a great green Moth with moon-light-coloured wings will flutter past. Hold out your hand and whisper softly: 'Moon Moth, may I go with you to the Land of Nod?' If he lights upon your hand, then you may follow him."

Tommy-Anne clasped her hands and looked up at the sky, with a little smile of deep content. This smile meant also gratitude, for she was very grateful.

"A few more questions; may I ask a very few more?" she said shyly, as if afraid that even an Oak might grow tired of *whys*.

"With pleasure," it answered, "if they are about trees. The fact is I am very young and have not had time to learn much, but of course I know all the history of our best tree families."

" Well, Mr. Rattle, what have you to say?" —p. 33.

32

"Thank you, dear patient little Oak! I will put some sticks around you, so that no one shall crush you until you grow big enough to stand by yourself. You fell from the great Oak above; but how did the other trees, that I see in the grass, come here? I am sure that there are no others with leaves like theirs, nearby."

"Pr-r-r-r-ink! Pr-r-r-ink. Pr-u-p! Pr-u-p! Pr-r-r-ink," chattered a voice from a branch of the great Oak that reached over Tommy-Anne's head. She knew before looking up that it was Adjidaumo, the Red Squirrel, who was talking and scolding.

There he sat, his tail curved up over his back, his round ears twitching, his poppy eyes gazing several ways at once, while he munched at a bunch of apple blossoms that he held between his front paws.

"Pr-r-r-ink! Pr-r-r-r-r!" he called again, turning suddenly about, so that he faced her.

"Well, Mr. Rattle, what have you to say? Do you know how the seeds of the other trees came here," she asked, shaking her finger at him, for they were old friends.

"Certainly I do; that is, of a part of them at least. I live in a hole under this tree, and my nest is up in the cedar yonder; and often when I've been to market over in the hickories above the river, or in the chestnuts behind the mill, and carry a great load home, I drop some of the nuts, and they grow.

"I don't think you know how hard I have to work sometimes, mistress, to get in our winter store of food. I carried four quarts of chestnuts, two nuts at a time, from over the river, and that wicked little dog of yours chased me every time I crossed your garden wall."

"He isn't a wicked dog; father says it is his nature to chase little beasts for food."

"Yes, for *food*. We all may take what we need to eat. Heart of Nature allows that. But Waddles is never *really* hungry; he has learned bad habits of the House People, and chases for sport, to see us run, as they do. We understand what hunger is and know all its excuses, but our law is like the Red Brother's, — 'take what ye need to eat.'

"Many a weary run I've had across the open, half choking, with my cheeks stuffed out with nuts, the dog behind, and not a tree to save me. One thing comforts me; I've dropped so many chestnuts on the way that a forest will surely grow there to shelter my great-grandchildren. Pr-r-r-r-ut! Pr-r-ink!" laughed Rattle.

"You brought me further than from the mill woods," said a thin, piping voice. "I sprouted two years ago, and I was *so* lonely, but I'm very thin and small, hardly bigger than my brothers of this spring."

"Who are *you?*" said Tommy-Anne. "Are you a tree? You and your brothers look like little whisps of moss."

"A tree? of course I am, and a very important tree too; — a Christmas tree, — or at least my mother was." And the little Spruce paused proudly, as if nothing more could be said in its praise.

"Then you must have come from Wild Cat Mountain; Christmas trees do not grow any nearer," she replied, looking down with great respect at the few dark green bristles that represented the tree.

"Yes, our family has lived there for centuries; I was a seed in a cone that Rattle brought home; he stripped it and ate all the other seeds, then dropped the cone, thinking it finished; that is why there is only *one* of me. Last year cones were in plenty. Rattle was careless, and scattered so many about here that now I have many companions."

"They do not grow as the Oak did; they have six little green fingers instead of leaves."

"Certainly, our family follows its own customs. Every respectable plant family has its own habits, shape, and colours. In some the leaves are broad, in some narrow; in some the veins run up and down, and in others across, like spider webbing (you will learn our laws in the Flower Market). In one thing we are all alike;—We all have roots, and we come from the spark of life that our mothers pack into the seed lunch baskets."

"Oh, oh! I see," said Tommy-Anne; "the food that Rattle finds in the nuts and cones was packed away to feed the plant life while it grew.

"But if I were you, little Spruce, I would rather stay out in the wood and grow tall, so that I could see over the hills to salt water, than be cut down for a Christmas tree when I was quite young."

"Tommy-Anne, have you never *seen* a Christmas tree, that you should talk so? The Snow Owl has seen one! He told my grandmother about it, and our family have never since complained when House People come and cut our brethren down after the first snow. He saw it in the great house in the village, the one where people go on Sundays, wearing their best clothes. The house that points up to the sky with one

long, white finger. The
Owl was roosting in a Yew
tree outside a window, when
a bright light shone out into
the dark, and he was about
to fly away, fearing some
trap or magic, when he
saw inside this house one
of our family all blooming
with such flowers as the
Snow Owl never saw before.
He said the tree bore gold and
silver fruit instead of dingy cones, and

that a great star, bigger than Sirius, the winter
watchman, hung on the top, and that lights more
brilliant than the fires of the north spangled the
branches. Then he said that House People and
their children came and sang songs to the tree
and did it homage. He promised to come back
and tell us more, if ever he could go inside the
house and see it closer."

"You dear little Spruce! *I* have a Christmas
tree every year; and now that I understand the
speech of Whyland, I will invite the Snow Owl
and all his friends to come and see it lighted."

Rattle grew jealous of the attention the tree
was receiving and began to chatter again. Just

then a fine blue bird, with a pointed cap and black collar, flew near, crying in a harsh voice, "Jay, Jay!" as if anxious to tell his name, and dropped on the branch close to Rattle, who was beginning to eat a fresh bunch of apple blossoms.

"Egg sucker!" screamed the Jay.

"Nut thief!" chattered the Squirrel, humping his back with rage.

"Where are my four fine fresh eggs?" shrieked the bird.

"Where are my first quality beech nuts?" squeaked the Squirrel. And without more ado they began to fight desperately.

"Stop, you horrid things!" called Tommy-Anne, resolutely. "You are both wrong. Father says people mostly are when they fight, and that they do it because they can't make excuses even to themselves.

"Stop this minute, or I will tell the butcher-boy where you live, and he will hunt you away. *He* can find anything, even a Hummingbird's nest."

This dreadful threat ended the quarrel, and the fighters began very meekly to explain; but another voice coming from the grass said, "The Jay did *not* steal the nuts; he gathered them himself from the top of the great Beech tree on the

lawn. I ought to know, because I am one of them
that he dropped."

"Yes, we are some that he dropped," said all
the little Beech trees in chorus.

"Then," said Rattle, bowing
politely to the Jay, with one
hand on his heart, "I will
say that *I* did *not* suck
your eggs. It was Kaw-
Ondaig, the lame-winged
Crow, who did it. I saw him
this morning when I was
leaping through the treetops
for exercise. But you need not make such a
fuss about it, Tchin, for you know those eggs
would never have hatched, because you and your
wife let them grow cold yesterday, while you
were worrying that Warbler who wished to build
on the ground under your tree. Poor Kaw is
old and feeble and cannot go out with the flock
down to the cornfields, or over to the shore for
mussels. Think twice before you try to make a
fight over bad eggs, friend Tchin!"

Tommy-Anne asked the Jay, after he had
grown quiet, if he could introduce her to any
birds of his acquaintance and tell her where
they nested. He, however, seemed to be very

uncomfortable, and after hesitating a long time said : —

"Mistress Tommy-Anne, the fact is I am not very popular with my tribe ; they suspect me of sometimes meddling with their nests, and so keep their secrets from me. One thing I do know, however: to-morrow is an anniversary day in Bird-land. Be early in the meadow between the river and wood, and you will see and hear enough, I promise you. Be early, mind ! " And Tchin (which was the Red Brother's name for him) flew away silently enough, as he can when he wishes.

" Aren't you ashamed of yourself now ? " said Tommy-Anne to Rattle.

"Not a bit, not a bit! *Somebody* stole my nuts," he blustered.

" You were both wrong," she continued; "for you could not prove what you said ; and by the way, pray why are you eating those apple blossoms ? "

" I need variety, missy, the same as the House People. Nuts are my meat, but sometimes I like a fresh egg or a flower salad." And he continued munching the fleshy base of the blossoms that would some day have grown into apples.

" For shame ! Rattle, I shall make you move away if you act so. Father will not let any one rob nests or hurt *anything* on his land; do you hear, sir?"

"Look at Waddles! look at Waddles!" cried Rattle, half in surprise and half to divert attention from himself.

Indeed, Waddles seemed to be very sad and quite spent. He was coming up the slope painfully and completely out of breath, his tongue hanging out, his head down. Great bunches of burdock seeds fringed his tail, making it look like a bit of frayed rope, while his usually smooth white coat was rough and muddy, and his black and tan ears gray with dust.

Tommy-Anne ran to meet him, half sorry and half inclined to scold. "Was the ham bone good?" she asked. "Eating it seems to have been very hard work. Or perhaps you have been burying it in a safer place out of the cat's reach. You know Tiger can dig very deep, and her claws are *very* sharp."

"I didn't eat the ham," gasped Waddles, between his pantings. "Tiger has it; she is a terrible cat, almost as big as a cow, and her claws are as long as pitchforks." Here he lifted his lovely little face to show deep scratches on his nose.

"You poor dear!" moaned Tommy-Anne, hugging him. "I'm sorry for your nose; but the next time you won't *steal* ham and have to hide it in an out-of-the-way place for Tiger's benefit, will you?

"Think," said she; "I have heard part of a secret since you have been away, and I can't know the whole of it until to-morrow. Tchin, the Jay, said, 'Be in the meadow between the river and the woods *very early*.'

"Remember, Waddles! very early! Oh, what if it should rain!"

Boom! boom! sounded the dinner gong down at the house. Waddles brightened up and cocked his ears so suddenly that Tommy-Anne laughed outright, and said mockingly: "So you wish some dinner; I thought that perhaps you would rather stay here and wait for Tiger to bring the ham bone back.

"No, you would rather come with me? Then wash your face and make yourself a bit tidy."

The dog began obediently to lick his paw and make a sponge of it to clean his smutty nose.

Boom! bang! but this time the sound was followed by a clear, melodious whistle.

" Hurry, Waddles; don't prink any more; don't
you hear the whistle? Father and mother have
come home early; *now* there may be pudding *and*
cake for dinner." She answered the call with a
shrill yoh-yoh-yoh cry, that was a combination of
Screech Owl and Indian war-whoop, — a sound that
had been very useful to her more than once when
she was lost in the far-away woods, — and then
hurried to the house, turning Tchin's words " To-
morrow early " into a merry song.

III

COCK ROBIN'S COUSINS

THAT night it rained. The Sun was sulky and out of sorts when it went down, and whispered crossly to Mudjekeewis, the West Wind, who went about repeating it among the trees on Wild Cat Mountain, scolding and jostling them until the great pines shook with rage.

The clouds rolled uneasily, the fierce winds of the upper air meddled, and tossed them hither and thither until they bumped into each other recklessly, and at every bump they growled like drums. The House People said, "Hear the thunder." Angry sparks flashed from between the clouds, streaking down the sky, forking and blazing like molten metal in the forge mould.

The time between the flash and the blows grew shorter, and the House People said, " The storm is coming nearer; see the lightning ! "

A few big drops of rain fell to try how dry the ground was. The earth sent up a little whiff of dust and cried, " Come, I am thirsty ! " and the rain shook itself from the grasp of the clouds.

Tommy-Anne sat on her father's knee by the open study window. Waddles had tipped over the scrap basket and curled himself up in it, at the first peal of thunder. His nerves were sadly upset by his encounter with the cat, and the lightning reminded him of the glare of her eyes. The glass eyes in the bearskin rug on the floor winked knowingly at him, and he was afraid that Aunt Prue might ask more questions about the ham, and altogether he thought wisely that " out of sight is out of mind."

" Whip-poor-will ! Whip-poor-will ! Whip-poor-will ! " called a voice close outside the window.

Tommy-Anne, half sleepy, started and clasped both her arms around her father's neck, while Waddles jumped out of the basket and bayed dismally, her mother, who was knitting something soft and white in the twilight, laughed and said, "So you are both afraid of a bird, though you spend all your days in the woods?"

"A bird! I didn't know that it was a bird," replied Tommy-Anne, regretfully; "I've never heard it before."

"No, dear," said her father; "we were not here while it was in song last season, and it is late in coming this year."

"In song? Doesn't it sing all the time? Where does it come from, and what is its name?"

"Few birds sing all the year; this one has come now from the south, and its name is the Whip-poor-will."

"Why doesn't it sing all the time, and why does it ever go away, and why is its name Whip-poor-will?" she asked in one breath.

"I will tell you the story about it that I heard when I was a little boy. There was a very poor woman who lived in a hut on the edge of a great forest, and all the money she could earn was by selling the bundles of dry sticks that she gathered. She had one child, a little boy named Will, and an old brown dog called Jock.

"Every day when she went down to the village to sell her sticks, Will would go to the wood to pick up more faggots, taking Jock for company.

One day the butcher gave her a piece of meat, and the baker a piece of dough, because she always brought a good measure of sticks, and she hurried home with the treasures, for they very seldom had meat at the hut.

"Next day, bright and early, she made a fine meat pie, baked it a delicious brown, and put it on the shelf for supper. Leaving a slice of bread and a lump of cheese on the table for her boy's dinner, she shouldered her load of sticks and tramped off to the village.

"It was a cool day in the early May, and when Will came home it was afternoon, and he was very hungry. He lighted a few sticks and made a little blaze on the hearth, then looked about for his food. He found a bowl of cold porridge in the closet. This he divided evenly between himself and Jock and then ate the bread and cheese. Still he was very hungry; he smelled the pie on the shelf and lifted it down to the table, intending only to look at it. He did not realize that his mother was walking all day, with only a slice of bread for luncheon, or how faint and tired she would be at night. He only remembered that *he* was hungry *then*.

"A bad little Puk-Wudjie, named Did-Not-Think, who causes a great deal of needless trouble, came in at the window, perched on the edge of the pie, and threw dust in his eyes, so that right and wrong became mixed up to him, though these mischievous spirits never come un-invited. 'I will take out one little piece of meat,' he said, — 'only one.' And he slipped his stout knife between the crust and the dish.

"It tasted so good, he took another piece. Did-Not-Think threw some more dust, and Will took a third piece, and another, and another.

"Suddenly the crust broke and dropped into the dish; he had eaten all the meat! Then another Puk-Wudjie, with a long face like a grasshopper, climbed to the edge of the dish. This one's name was Didn't-Mean-To. He whimpered a little and then whispered, 'The pie is spoiled now, so you might as well eat the crust.' So Will ate it, and there remained only the dish with a third Puk-Wudjie sitting in the bottom of it, crying and rubbing his eyes with his knuckles; and this one's name was So-Sorry. Then all three began to point at Will, and sing together, 'What will your mother *say* to you? What will your mother *do* to you?'

" Will was now very much ashamed of what he had done, as well as somewhat frightened, and he ran out of the hut up to the forest ; but Jock remained asleep on the hearth.

" It was almost dark when the poor woman came home, thinking of the nice pie, and of how she and her boy would have a feast. She lighted a candle and looked on the shelf for the pie. ' I thought that I left it there,' she said. ' No ! I was mistaken ; it is on the table.'

" The candle flickered, and she did not see very well ; but when she came nearer she discovered the empty dish. Looking about, she noticed that Will was gone, while Jock was in the house.

" ' You wicked dog,' she said, ' to eat our supper, while my poor boy is hard at work in the woods ! ' And she beat Jock with the broom and turned him out of doors.

" Meanwhile, Will was wandering in the woods, feeling very wretched, and thinking about what his mother would say, and wondering how she would punish him.

" ' Whip-poor-will ! Whip-poor-will ! Chur-rk ! ' said a loud voice, directly above him. For a moment he was so startled he could not move.

" ' Whip-poor-will ! Whip-poor-will ! Chu-r-r-k ! '

E

it cried, the last word sounding like a switch
striking the air.

"Will darted from one tree to another, but the
voice always followed, and in despair he ran home,
the bird following close behind him and calling in

at the door of the
hut. And though
she did not like to
do it, his mother
whipped him ; for
she said the bird
knew best, and
poor Jock had been
punished for noth-
ing. This bird
has been called
the Whip-poor-
will ever since, and
when the woods-
men hear him, they say, 'Some one hereabout
has done wrong.'"

During the last part of the story Waddles
sneaked out of the room. "He feels guilty about
that ham bone," laughed Tommy-Anne to herself.

The bird called again, four or five times in suc-
cession, this time from the end of the garden.

" Father dear, *please* let me go and look for him,"
she pleaded, knowing very well that it was bed-
time. Unfortunately for her the tall clock began
to whirr, and then gave eight deliberate strokes.

" No, little Owl ; don't you know that everything is soaking with the rain? Wait until to-
morrow ; it will be a fine day for all your bird
friends after this shower; then you may take your
luncheon and stay out all day." So she went contentedly to bed after pushing her comfortable
little nest nearer to the window so that she might
be sure to wake early.

" Whip-poor-will ! " called the bird once more,
brushing the window glass in his circling. Quick
as a flash she was up, and opening the window a
crack, thrust her head out, calling, " Good-night,
Whip-poor-will ; do you feel as lonely as you
sound? and will you be at the anniversary to-
morrow ? "

" Yes ; I shall be there, Tommy-Anne, and I
don't feel sad a bit. I'm very merry, in fact; the
people who tell stories about me do not understand my language ; that is all."

Then she heard voices in the next room, which
was the study, — her Aunt Prue talking to her parents. " If she were mine," the voice said sharply,
" I would stop such antics. There she is standing

in her nightgown, talking out of the window to
nothing." Her mother only said, "It is a very
warm night, sister Prue," but her father sighed
and began to write, saying, "It were well if
we all could be as close to the Heart of Nature as
she is."

"Father knows Heart of Nature, my dear Tree
Man, so everything must be all right," whispered

Tommy-Anne, in ecstasy. "Then he must know
the other Hearts too. I'm *so* glad ! *Remember to-
morrow early*," she whispered, as she curled down
on her pillow. When everything was quite still,
Waddles crept in and rested from his unhappy
day on his special piece of carpet, keeping one eye
upon the bed, where his mistress usually found him
in the morning, though it was against the rules.

Gheezis, the Sun, was thinking of getting up,

and like many another important person, made a great fuss about the matter.

First he called the gray night clouds that hung about his path, telling them to go and sweep the sky clean ; so they sailed up higher and higher in long ridges, collecting all the little cloud scraps as they went. Then he called to the white river mists, that hang low and heavily over the ponds and streams, " Come that I may drink," — and as they arose, he swallowed them one by one.

Then Gheezis looked up over the edge of the part of the earth that can be seen at one time, which the House People call the horizon, and all the sky flushed red with pleasure. Only Wabun Annung, the Morning Star, turned pale, and the shadows slipped away, except those that hid behind trees where Gheezis did not look. The Puk-Wudjies, the little wood folk that live in the brown-tented toadstool villages, vanished in their homes, and Suggema, the Mosquito, came out of the marsh, wiping the dew from his long nose and began to sing, wending his zigzag way upward to the pastures; and Mudjekeewis came smiling from his pleasure palace.

"Say, say! What's the row? I'm awake, so are you," jeered Miou, the gray Catbird, tipping his black-capped head on one side and flicking his tail.

"Winter's over, winter's over! Hear me laughing, laughing, — see!" sang the black and white Bobolink, soaring high above the meadow grass.

Tommy-Anne started, rubbing her eyes, saw that the sun had risen some time ago, heard the bird music, and then scolded Waddles, who had found his way, as usual, to the foot of her bed, and was waking very slowly, yawning and making a bow of his back.

"Oh, Waddles, Waddles! I told you to remind me, — 'to-morrow early,' — and it's late now, and there's bath and breakfast before we can go out. I could take my breakfast in my pocket, but not my bath. I wonder if the anniversary has begun." And she hung out of the window, looking anxiously toward the meadow, which could not be seen because of the trees.

A tiny brown Wren, wild with good spirits,

chattered at her from the honeysuckle. "Perhaps he will tell me something about it," she said.

"Tell you something about what?" he answered pertly, never stopping his nervous hopping from twig to twig. "What do you want to know — who I am? I'm Johnny Wren; I live here in this little box; soon there will be spotted brown eggs in it — perhaps five — perhaps ten — who knows — do you? If we like it here — and no cats come — we'll stay — make another nest in the next box later on. New nest for every brood — best way — more neat — some birds don't, though — we are neat — are you? Here comes my wife — hear her scold — good-bye!"

"Now I know what a chatterbox is," said Tommy-Anne, drawing a long breath. "He asked us if we are neat, Waddles. Perhaps he was hinting about that bath. I think I had better set about it, because it's a *must be*, that only stops for two things, — a bad cold and frozen water pipes."

Tommy-Anne and her father had their breakfast together on a little table in the piazza, and Tommy-Anne poured out his coffee and carried it to him as steadily as if she was not eager to be down in the meadow. They often breakfasted together in this way, for her mother was not very strong and slept late, and Aunt Prue simply would *not* take a meal out of doors. "Dining-rooms are to eat in," she said ; "if one is to eat with bugs and ants crawling over the butter, and flies in the milk, one might as well be a pedlar and live in a cart."

A Robin flew past, calling, "Quick ! Quick !" It was only his fussy way, but Tommy-Anne thought that he was telling her to hurry; and her father, seeing her earnestness, let her go, first asking if she had on her thick boots.

Yes, she had ; for thick boots were her dear friends, and a *why* that she thoroughly understood, after a summer spent in the company of ankles bruised with stones and striped with briar scratches, to say nothing of colds.

"We are too late, Waddles; I'm sure we are too late," she sighed, as they crossed the bridge, and standing under a great apple tree, the be-

ginning of the old orchard, looked over the
meadow toward the woods. "The Boholinks
are here, but they always are; they make flat pie
nests in the grass. I stepped in one last summer;
but lucky for them it was empty. They are too
giddy to tell us anything. As soon as they see
any one coming, they sail straight up in the air
and sing so fast that they forget the words and
have to come down again to think."

"Mistress," said Waddles, who had been sniffing where the grass was trampled down in a
long trail, "the Miller's bull, Taw, is out for a
walk *without* the Miller. Now the last time Taw
went walking alone a great many accidents happened. My particular friend, the Doctor's dog,
Flo, sprained her back, our pasture fence fell
over, and the Egg Woman, who was going across
lots to the store, spilled four dozen fresh eggs and
had to climb up this very tree that we are standing under, in an awful hurry.

"When the Miller came to find the bull,
Taw roared at him terribly from over the river,
and shook his brass nose-ring, saying 'I'm out
for the day,'—and so he was. For the Miller
knows that there is no use in contradicting a bull
in an open field, when there is no rope tied to his
nose-ring. I think, mistress, that you had better

climb this apple tree *now*, for there is a queer noise over in the wood." So saying, Waddles made himself into a very small package behind the gnarled trunk, where he could see and not be seen.

There certainly was a commotion in the wood. Birds were chattering at a great rate, not singing, but giving their call notes and alarm cries.

" The anniversary must be beginning," said Tommy - Anne, from her perch ; " don't you want to come where you can see better, Waddles? I can pull you up, and there is a nice wide branch for you to sit on, if you keep quite still."

" No thank you; it's against the custom of our family to climb trees. I might be disgraced by being mistaken for a cat. Look quick, mistress ! "

The clamour was coming nearer. Swallows darted above the river, whispering excitedly. Robins flew from tree to bush, calling hurriedly. A flame-coloured Oriole shot over, and perching in the old apple tree above Tommy-Anne's head, gave some notes like a bugle call. Down from the woods came a strange procession of birds : hundreds and hundreds of them ; some walking, some flying close above the ground, — but all keeping in groups of a colour or a family, like the companies of a regiment, led by a large Owl walking between a Thrush and a Crow.

So many birds moving at once made Tommy-Anne almost dizzy, and she looked up to ask the Oriole what it all meant, when she saw that he had left the tree, and a dark gray bird, who was bowing and trying to attract her attention, was in his place. "Say, say !" it called — " Prut, prut, — say, say ! hi, hi ! victory !" It was Miou, the Catbird.

"Good-morning," cried Tommy-Anne, in delight. " You are the very person I wanted to see, because you are always so sociable, and seem to really enjoy telling what you know."

"Good-morning," he piped gaily, for he felt very much complimented by being called a person. " Good-day, good-day ! excuse me for not taking off my cap, but I can't, you see, because *it grows on.*" And he laughed at his own little joke.

"Now, Miou," said Tommy-Anne, "please tell me about the anniversary, and where all those birds came from." And she pointed at the procession that was fast breaking up into little parties that explored the meadow and neighbouring orchard.

"Don't you really know about them? They are coming from Cock Robin's funeral."

"Cock Robin's funeral!" she cried, in amazement. "I thought that he was an English Robin, and that he died years ago. I heard about it when I was *very* young, I am sure."

"So he was, so he did," chattered Miou, delighted to have a listener. "It is not the real funeral, but the anniversary of it, that we celebrate. We are his kinsmen, you know; and we do it to make us remember that we have declared war against the English Sparrow who killed him.

> "'Who killed Cock Robin?'
> 'I' said the Sparrow;
> 'With my bow and arrow
> I killed Cock Robin.'"

sang Miou, softly.

"I never thought of that before," said Tommy-Anne, "and I've often wondered why the Spar-

rows were always fighting with other birds.   I
suppose that is why people celebrate anniver-
saries of battles and things, so that they can
remember to feel angry; and birthdays for fear
they shall forget how old they are.   Only,
Miou, have you noticed that some people don't
seem to have any birthdays?   That must be
because they want to forget."

The bird began to look bored, as talkative
people are apt to when some one else is speaking, and seemed anxious to go on with his story.

"Pray excuse me," said Tommy-Anne; "but
at the real funeral the bull tolled the bell.
How do you manage that?"

"That is quite a long story," said Miou, contentedly settling himself on his twig.   "For
years and years we *imagined* the bull, — left a
place for him in the procession and played that
he was there, you know.   This year, Dahinda,
the greatest Bull-frog in the pond, told Wawa,
the Wild Goose, who was swimming near him,
that our anniversary was getting to be very
dull, and that he had heard the birds say, when
they were bathing, that they would stop coming to it if there was not more variety.

"Wawa asked him what he could suggest,
and Dahinda said, 'Have a real bull in the pro-

cession,' and kept on saying, ' B-u-ll ! B-u-ll ! ' all day, until the Council of Birdland agreed with him.

" That was the beginning of trouble. We all knew Taw, the Miller's bull, very well, and Ko-ko-ko-ho, the Horned Owl, who sleeps near the barn, promised to invite him. Taw said he would be happy to come, but did not know how he could get out alone, unless the Council could make a plan. So they appointed the Owl, the Jay, the Wood Dove, and the Wren a committee of arrangement to do the work. They chose the Owl because he looked wise ; the Jay, because he was not troubled with too many scruples ; the Dove, because he agreed with almost every one ; and the Wren, because he was energetic. Tchin, the Jay, who promised to get Taw out, asked his friend, the Red Fox, to run swiftly through the barnyard early in the morning, when the Miller's boy was leading Taw to the water-trough. So far all went well. The boy dropped the rope that was fastened in Taw's nose-ring, to chase the Fox, and Taw pushed open the gate and came to us."

" Where did you get the bell for him to toll, and where is he now ? " said Tommy-Anne, unable to resist asking questions ; " he did not come back with the procession."

"You go too fast; give me time," said Miou. "We had to *imagine* the bell because we hadn't any, and if we had one, the noise would have told the Miller exactly where Taw was and spoiled everything."

"Of course!" ejaculated Tommy-Anne. "Half the *whys* would answer themselves if they took time to think. But where is Taw now?"

"Ah!" said Miou; "that is the trouble. After the celebration, when he should have come back with us to this tree to hear the stories and songs — "

"Stories? what stories?" cried she.

"After the anniversary we always have a feast, and sing, and tell stories about where we have spent the winter; for it is the first time that we have all met since last year. It is very interesting."

"Shall I hear these stories?" said Tommy-Anne, her eyes dancing with pleasure.

"I don't think, by the way you interrupt *me*, that you *wish* to hear stories," said Miou, severely.

"Please forgive me," she begged; "but Heart of Nature said that I might ask questions of all the things *themselves*, so that I could learn a great many *whys*."

"That is different," said Miou, and then added suspiciously, "Do you know the pass-word?"

"Yes; it is Brotherhood!" she replied promptly.

"Very good. Now to go back to Taw. After we had imagined that we had buried Cock Robin, and were starting to return through the wood, one of those bad Cowbirds, who have nothing to do but meddle and gossip, perched on Taw's back and whispered in his ear, 'There's fine fall grain over the other way; fresh green eating. Come see,' and went walking off to show the way, Taw following. We were all well frightened, and the Council ordered the Committee of Management to bring Taw back.

"Ko-ko-ko-ho would do nothing about it, because he is a night owl, and he says the light hurts his eyes; Tchin, the Jay, said he had only agreed to bring Taw *out, not* get him *back*. The Dove tiptoed and said nothing, and the Wren tried to argue with Taw, who only laughed at her, and she flew away threatening to call the Miller.

"Meanwhile, Taw is eating all the beautiful young wheat, and we are sorry, because it belongs to the Blacksmith, and he is very good to us and keeps the boys from robbing our nests hereabouts, and feeds those of us who stay all winter."

"It was very wrong in Taw to act so," said Tommy-Anne, sympathetically.

"Who says that Taw is wrong?" roared a deep voice under the tree.

Miou gave a few startled flips with his wings, and Tommy-Anne drew up her feet suddenly and took a firmer hold of the branch, for below stood Taw, shaking his head and pawing up the thick sod angrily : he had waded up the river quite unseen.

Waddles, making himself very narrow indeed, peeped from behind the tree with one eye, on the alert for any sudden movement of the bull, and all the birds gathered near, covering the old fence and huddling in the apple tree.

Tommy-Anne knew that the tree was strong and safe and she was very anxious to hear how Taw had been persuaded to return, and so ventured to question him.

"Don't be angry, Taw. I said it was wrong to eat the grain when the birds had been kind enough to ask you to their anniversary. Did the Wren coax you to come back?"

"Johnny Wren? Poof," snorted Taw. "The birds were selfish; they expected me to walk in their procession and then go home before the feast. Now that I have had *my* feast, I am going home because I *wish* to." And Taw marched slowly up hill toward the barn, switching his tail and dragging his rope behind him.

The birds were so surprised and ashamed at what Taw said, that they hung their heads in silence. But Waddles, who had noticed that Taw looked anxious in spite of his indifference, called out, "Johnny Wren *did* make him come back; look, mistress, the Miller and the Butcher's boy and the Butcher are coming from the wood. Bulls do not like butchers."

For half an hour the birds feasted on everything that they liked best.

Then one by one the birds plumed themselves and settled in the apple tree or nearby bushes, according to their habit. All who had taken part in the procession did not remain, because the nesting season was well under way, and that means serious business to a bird; but every family left some delegates to hear the stories.

" Have you always met here ? " Tommy-Anne asked of Miou.

" Not quite always, but for as long a time as I can remember. This tree is a part of a very old orchard where a great many of our mothers and grandmothers were hatched, and Heart of Nature tells us to come back to where we were born, when we are ready to make homes for ourselves. No matter how far he leads us in the winter, he always shows us the way back when the nesting time comes. Then this is a spot where we can all meet comfortably for our anniversary. Here we have shelter, water, and food. What more does Birdland need ? "

The Song-Sparrow who was the head of the Summer Council of Birdland, presently gave three soft notes and a trill, to call the birds together, and asked, " My brothers, what is your pleasure ? Shall we have music first or a story ? "

Miou came down from the high branch where Tommy-Anne was perching, and said, first bowing respectfully right and left : " Ladies and gentlemen (though I see that you are mostly gentlemen, as at this season your wives are necessarily busy), we have a House Child among us. Heart of Nature has lent her the Magic Spectacles, that she may see rightly many things in his farm and know our language. For his sake, let her choose what we shall do." And with one voice they consented.

Tommy-Anne felt very shy, as she slipped to a lower branch, to acknowledge the honour.

"You climb well," said the Nuthatch with the white vest, who was an acrobat. "Can you walk head down as I do?" taking a few steps in that position to illustrate his meaning.

"Oh no, I'm sure I could never do that," she replied, "though I used to crawl downstairs head first, when I was *very young*."

"What shall we do to give you pleasure, little House Child?" asked the Song-Sparrow, kindly.

"It is so very sudden that I hardly know what to say, but I would like to hear all that I can about Birdland. Why you come and go, and how you change your feathers; why some of you sing and others only call; and why there are so many kinds of nests. All the reasons and *whys*, you know," she added desperately, being very sure she was mixing things and afraid of forgetting what she wished to ask.

The Council spoke together in low tones for a

minute, and then the Song-Sparrow said: "We do not ourselves know *why* we do a great many things. We do them because Heart of Nature tells us to; but what we do know, that we will tell you willingly. Brothers, I must ask you to help in this. Bob o' Lincoln, will you tell of the comings and goings, and of the different coats and names you wear the year around?"

"Will I, won't I?" bubbled the Bobolink, soaring up from the grass; "I should think so! I can talk of it, sing of it, cry at it, laugh at it, all the summer. Hear me laughing-laughing-laughing-winters-over-winters-over-singing — singing — s-i-n-g-i-n-g!" And he shook little bells from his throat that tinkled off through the air.

Then said the Song-Sparrow: "Let the Robin speak for those of the garden and orchard; the valiant Kingbird, for the more silent birds of the air; the Oriole shall teach of the nest-building, for he is the prince of weavers."

"Who shall speak of the birds that sometimes eat *us*, their kinsmen?" whispered the Wood Dove, who always suggested something disagreeable in the most plausible manner possible.

All the birds turned pale and looked up through the trees, half expecting to see a Hawk hovering in the sky.

"Yes, I must hear about the cannibal birds," said Tommy-Anne, eagerly.

"If you must, you must," said the Song-Sparrow, regretfully ; "but it is not a story for a day like this, for we do not like to hear such tales. Ko-ko-ko-ho shall tell it to you, when the days grow cold. Ko-ko-ko-ho will tell it wisely ; he knows the ways of these birds, and the House People do not always judge rightly of the matter."

"The championship! when shall we sing for the championship?" cried Miou, anxiously. "Who sings this year?"

"The Catbird, the Meadowlark, and the Oriole," said Ma-ma, the black and white Woodpecker, who was the Secretary, and kept the records of Birdland neatly written with his bill on the tree bark, in letters of his own fashioning. In fact, you may see these annals traced in strange characters on many trees.

"Then let us have a story, and after the story a song," said Tommy-Anne.

"Mistress," said Waddles, as he turned round three times, to make a nice bed in the grass before he lay down, "how about dinner?"

"I forgot to say," interrupted the Song-Sparrow, who overheard this remark, "that we always

adjourn from eleven to four, as few self-respect-
ing birds care to talk or sing *all* day."

"How about me? how about me?" ejaculated
the little olive Vireo with the red eyes, who
never ceases talking, or working from sunrise
to sunset. "Am I no one?"

"I said *few*, not *none*," answered the Song-
Sparrow, soothingly.

"Mistress," said Waddles again, "I think at
this rate we shall have to stay out all night."

"Hush-h-h!" called half a dozen birds; "the
Bobolink is ready."

IV

SNAKES IN THE GRASS

THE Bobolink balanced himself on a long blackberry cane, which swayed to and fro with his
weight. He had great difficulty in keeping right
side up, and made several little excursions into
the air, before he alighted to his complete satis-
faction.

Finally the audience began to grow impatient
at his antics, so Bob flew over, and after making
sure that his feathers were quite smooth, began : —

"My story is for our guest, the House Child ;

and you must pardon me, my brothers, if I repeat much that you already know.

"I am a happy-go-lucky bird with two coats, a very masquerader, so that many House People think that I am several birds and give me many names, — Bobolink, Reedbird, Butterbird, Ricebird. Did any one say rice? I dote on rice!

"I come northward in the spring-time wearing my shining black dress-coat, with buff and white facings. I sing all day long above the meadows where my nest is hidden. They then call me Bobolink, Robert of Lincoln, and many other fanciful names. They watch me fly aloft, they rave about my voice and try to turn my songs into their words, while their singers make rhymes about me. Yet before the summer is over, my glossy coat drops away, feather by feather, and there falls over me a dusty cloak of beggar's brown, and with my shining feathers my voice is put away, save only a few notes.

"When the singing is over, then the dance begins, the dodging and the hiding; then House People harry us from cover to cover, calling us Reedbirds, kill and eat us, forgetting that we are the same Bobolinks who sang until they thought us bewitched. But these two, the singer and the scrap of food, are the same; only the poor southern gentleman is stripped of all his finery. Now it is May, the Moon of Leaves, the Moon of Nests, and here I am again. How I wish that it could be always May and always morning!

"Two months ago, in company with my brothers of the wing, I started from our winter home beyond the Amazon. We men left first, usually flying by night, in advance of the ladies, who are never quite ready for their journey; covering half a hundred miles in half a hundred minutes, then halting, resting, lounging, and feeding for days together."

"How did you know your way back here?"

"It is a long journey, but many birds travel still farther and make their flight in half the time that we take. As to finding the way,— even a madcap Bobolink knows the way back to the place where he first saw his mother flying to him with food, and learned to feel the strength of his wings. We don't have to think; we know!

"When we reached this America, the first of our battles with the House People began, the first and greatest. We were *so* hungry, after our long flight; *oh, so hungry!* And our chief food is seed food, and when we reached the south lands, the seed in the great rice fields

was sprouting. Rice is a word that makes us
forget everything, — rice, rice, rice! We, the
jolly, jostling troop, who had but recently shaken
off our winter coats, and day by day were
polishing the last flecks of rust from our new
feathers.

"Our hunger and the means we took to quell
it soon became the cause of battle. Heart of
Nature says, 'Take what ye need for food.' Did
we need to be told this twice, with the fields of
sprouting rice below us?

"The House People said, 'This is *our* food; you
shall not have it.' Now, *shall not* are reckless
words to hurl at gallant Southern gentlemen;
so we did not obey, but ate the more, — in fact,
we gobbled!

"Then, for nights and days, the House People
walked around the fields, making a great din to
frighten us away, building fires, waving strange
things, and pointing at us with pop-sticks that
spit the sharp killing wind that all birds dread.
And though we left many comrades on this battle-
field, they were but few compared to those who,
well filled with rice, continued their journey.

"Further up we flew, until we reached the
middle of these States, south of which we build
no nests. Here and there, parties broke away

from the main flock and scattered to their different birthplaces, and we grew hoarse from signalling. I waited here with some comrades until the flocks of females came, while others went still northward."

" Why don't you choose your mates before you start? I should think it would make the journey more cheerful," said Tommy-Anne.

" That would never do. Suppose that I chose a wife who was born in the far north; she could not stop here in your meadow, but would fly on, and then I should have had all my trouble for nothing."

" I thought that some birds stayed mated all their lives, like people," said Tommy-Anne.

" So they do; a great many of us keep the same mate, but we woo her over again every spring; it's safer never to take anything for granted, and it's much more fun besides. Some birds who can find food and lodging in nearly the same place at all seasons, or at most do not travel far, stay together all the year. Wawa knows a pair of Ospreys that have been mated for more than forty years, nesting on the same spot on a sea-island every summer. He told about it last year at the anniversary, and Ko-ko-ko-ho said he knew that it was true.

"Heart of Nature has arranged that we far-flying birds shan't mate until we reach our nesting-grounds. So we have a merry, careless time as we fly along, knowing that the right mate will be sure to follow. After I came here I won my wife, who is now hidden so safely down in the meadow grasses that not one of you can find her. She is not my last year's mate, however, for that one died from having too much confidence in House People."

"Shall I try to find your wife?" said Waddles, jumping up and sniffing the air eagerly. "I think that she is calling you now."

"So she is! dear me, so she is!" ejaculated

Bob. "No, I thank you; don't trouble yourself, I'll see what she wants. I had forgotten when I said that no one could find her, that *you* were near. Excuse me a moment; she is flying this way." So saying, he spread his wings, and floated down to where a sober brown bird was giving cries of distress.

"Is *that* Bob's wife?" asked Tommy-Anne of the Song-Sparrow; "she doesn't look a bit like him."

"Yes, that's Mrs. o' Lincoln. A great many mother birds wear different colours from their mates, as Bob will tell you. Look, House Child! — they are in trouble and are calling us." And all the birds began giving alarm cries, and darted in a body to the meadow. Tommy-Anne called Waddles and prepared to follow them.

"You had better take a stick or a stone, mistress," said Waddles. "I think that a snake is making all this fuss, and you never seem to like snakes."

Tommy-Anne seized a stout piece of fence rail and hurried after the birds; stepping carefully *over* the grass, which was fast growing long, instead of wading through it without looking, as was her habit.

The birds, with the exception of Ko-ko-ko-ho

and Oo-oo, were gathered in the low bushes, while several Kingbirds (the gray flycatchers with white breast and tail band, who dash boldly into the air after insects) were engaged in rising and then dropping with outspread wings upon some object in the grass, at which they struck violently. Mrs. o' Lincoln perched near by on a bit of stubble, wings drooping, beak open, while Bob was trying by every means in his power to coax her away.

As another Kingbird swooped, Tommy-Anne looked carefully in the grass and saw the head of a gray and brown mottled snake with a black and white belly, who was coiling and striking angrily at the bird. It was rather a thick snake, with a small head, and was perhaps three feet long, but it was hard to judge of its length, owing to the coils. It swung its head around and round, and darted its tongue, when the Kingbird came near, but never took its eyes from Mrs. o' Lincoln, who seemed to be paralyzed.

"Be careful, mistress," whispered Waddles; "there is another snake behind you, under that elder bush. Wake up Mrs. Bob, or you will fall."

Tommy-Anne felt very daring just then, and not at all afraid; besides, all the birds fell back when

she came, and evidently expected her to do something.

"Stop that, sir!" she called, aiming her stick
at the snake's head, but only succeeding in striking his tail. "Look at me and tell me what you
are trying to do. Stop worrying that poor bird!"

As the snake looked about for means of escape,
Mrs. o' Lincoln shook off her tremor and flew
to the brier beside her husband.

"Don't strike me again; I can explain," said
the snake, looking from side to side with that sly
glance that all things have who are perpetually
hunted and scorned, whether they are beasts or
people.

"Very well, you shall have a chance; but first
call your mate from under the bush, and if either
of you try to get away, I shall tell my dog to bite
you. Watch out, Waddles!"

Waddles gave a shiver and looked at his mistress, whispering, "Is that a real order, or the
kind that the Butcher's boy calls 'bluff'?"

"A real order," said his mistress aloud; and he
curled down close to her feet, his forehead wrin-
kling with anxiety as to which end of which snake
he would be expected to bite first.

"Now," said Tommy-Anne, as the snakes
straightened themselves out obediently before

her, " tell me your names, where you live, why you were frightening these birds, and if you are poisonous. You look to me like those horrid adders who sometimes puff themselves up."

" My name is Lac, and my wife is called Lactina," said the snake who had done the fighting. " We are not biting snakes, having no fangs or poison glands, nor are we even adders but an innocent pair of garden creatures. The House People call us milk-snakes because they think we go into their cellars for the milk they keep there ; but we are only hunting for mice that gather in such places, and never touch the milk.

" Ask the Puk-Wudjies ; they will tell you that we are harmless, and they come into our holes and huddle among our folds when Kabibonokka is abroad. We feed on mice, doing good, not harm ; for mice destroy the grain, the wood of houses, and all the roots of things."

" Humph ! " said Tommy-Anne ; " if you are garden snakes and live on mice, what are you doing in this meadow teasing birds ? "

Lac dropped his head and then replied, " There are no birds in that nest, but eggs only, though we do sometimes eat birds when we are hungry. Do the House People never eat birds ? "

Tommy-Anne felt very much embarrassed ; for

G

Waddles — who was pleased that Lac was excusing himself so that he would not have to be bitten — answered: "Yes, certainly, we killed chickens at our house yesterday, and I shall have some of the bones for my supper!"

"When we eat birds," said Tommy-Anne, "we kill them first.   You were thinking of swallowing poor Mrs. o' Lincoln alive, as I have seen the striped garter snake, who lives in our garden, swallow toads."

"No, no!" cried Lac and Lactina together; "we always kill first, so —" and Lac threw his coil around a twig, contracting his folds until it was crushed, saying proudly, "We are constrictors!"

"You have not told me yet what you are doing in this field when you belong in a garden," continued Tommy-Anne, desperately, feeling that she was getting the worst of the argument.

"People will not let us stay in their gardens," said Lactina, sorrowfully; "so we are looking about for field mice. If you will let us live in your garden wall, we will take good care of everything under ground."

"What good could you possibly do?"

"Eat all the mice that gnaw your flower bulbs, — your tulips, crocuses, and lilies, — that pinch the rose roots, letting the sap out. Mice do endless harm; but a garden that keeps a proper pair of snakes yields many flowers."

"If I let you live in our wall, will you promise never to touch our birds?"

"Yes," hissed Lac and Lactina, joyfully.

"Another thing," said Tommy-Anne: "will you promise *never* to come out suddenly or speak to me when I'm sitting on the wall?"

"Yes," they answered, beginning to glide away.

"One thing yet, Lac,— but this is for your good, — don't go into our dairy to look for *mice!* Aunt Prue always kills snakes, even if she has slippers on, and only a small broom to do it with!"

As the snakes slid off toward the garden, the birds returned to the apple tree, all talking at once, not a few of them finding fault with Tommy-Anne for not having killed Lac and Lactina.

"Mark my words, you'll rue it, rue it," scolded the Vireo.

"I have a fine nest in your biggest lilac bush," complained Miou. "I don't think it's fair to let those creepy things come so near."

"It is very disagreeable for our family, who always build near the ground," said the Song-Sparrow, mournfully.

"I thought you said that Heart of Nature wished all his people to have food," answered

Tommy-Anne, promptly; "you must complain to him about it. Perhaps the grasshopper that Tchin has this minute eaten, objects to *birds!* Please go on with your story, Bob; your wife is quite comfortable now. When you left off, you had told us that she was down in the grass. Please explain why she is so different from you in colour. Is it always so?"

"Yes, with us, we are the dandies who do all the dressing and the singing and sky-larking; our wives wear a brown striped gown all the year; and among many birds the feathers of the mates are different, and where a male has bright feathers his wife is usually of a dull colour."

"Why is that? I think the wife should have the finest dress."

"It's this way: if the mother bird, who sits the oftenest on the nest, wore gay feathers, her enemies would see her more readily; and the females are also usually smaller."

"Smaller! Speak for yourself," shouted Mrs. Ko-ko-ko-ho. "In *our* family it is different. I am two inches taller than my little husband over there in the wood, who prefers sleeping to improving his mind by listening to stories; and in the family of our cousins, the Hawks, the female is also the larger!"

"Wough, wough, wough!" barked Waddles, "I never took *you* for a Missis!" And he grinned from ear to ear, which, considering the size and shape of his mouth, was a very large grin indeed.

"Please excuse us, Bob, and go on; we have all been upset by the snakes," said Tommy-Anne.

So the Bobolink shifted his position a little and continued:—

"My wife and I have settled down to our family cares. I was born in this meadow, and she came from the marsh lands over the hill by salt water. As you see, we don't make much of a nest; a bunch of grass and a few twigs are enough to keep the eggs from rolling away. There my wife sits upon five eggs spotted with brown, and I sing to her to keep up her spirits, and also to let the world know how happy I am. Now I carry food to her; soon we shall take turns in carrying food to the young o' Lincolns. Why don't I sit on the nest? Oh no, I can't keep quiet a minute; it makes me giddy even to sit still while talking."

"What do they eat?" asked Tommy-Anne.

"At first all kinds of wee insects, even though their parents are seed-eaters. Insects are the milk that Birdland babies thrive best upon, for young birds must grow quickly and need strong nourishment."

" What colour are the young birds ? "

" Like their mother.   Heart of Nature gives
them all the dull colour in the beginning, that
they may be less easily seen while they are
learning to fly.

" I will tell you what we do after the young
leave the nest; at least, I will
speak of last year. *We* raised
two broods. My mate was a
gentle bird, but much too
trusting, and with no common sense ; she let the field
rats peer into her nest
without calling me, and
had no fear of House
People, hardly believ-
ing me when I said that
they set traps for us.

" After our young were raised,
even though it was full summer, Heart of Nature
reminded us that we had much to do before
Kabibonokka came.   Our feathers were worn and
broken from rubbing in the nest, so we retreated
among the reeds to moult our spring coats, and
at the same time our young changed their baby
feathers for stronger pinions.

" The new feathers that came in made us

striped brown alike, — father, mother, children.
A single call-note was all that was left of my
music, a sharp clink, like the striking together
of the shoes of a clumsy horse.

"For two months, more or less, we roved about
the lowlands, feeding on various seeds, and gain-
ing strength for our journey. Sometimes we had
fun; then it was stupid and panicky being driven
from marsh to marsh by the hunters, the sharp
wind from their pop-sticks blowing holes in a lot
of us; but my family remained together.

"A time came when I could not find my mate.
I looked everywhere in vain. I always knew that
something would surely happen to her. Our
time had come for leaving, early frosts were
cutting down our food,-and hosts of us had already gone to the rice fields. I went once more
to the meadow, where my nest still remained, a
sodden mass of sticks and grasses, thinking that
she might be there.

"Some House People were picking apples near
by, but I did not fear them, and my heart leaped
up, for close beside the fence I saw my mate sitting upon a brown, nest-like thing, her wings up-
raised as if to fly to me, only she did not move.

"I called; she did not answer. I flew down
and touched her with my beak; she did not stir.

I grasped her with my claws and gave her a shake, but she was bewitched and held fast to the brown straws upon which she was perching.

"The House People came toward the fence, and I flew to the wood edge and called the Puk-Wudjies, who teach us of the doings of the House People, imploring them to tell me what it all meant.

"They sent one of their scouts, called Reason-Why, to hear what the people said. Meanwhile a House Child picked up the thing to which my mate was fastened and put it on her head. I saw that it was the leaf that they wear to keep the sun off, called a hat.

"A man, with a kindly face, walked beside the little girl, and Reason-Why climbed on his shoe to hear what he was saying.

"'Where did you get that bird, little daughter?' he asked. 'I do not like to see you wearing such things. It is like a savage who decorates himself with the scalps from the heads of his neighbours.'

"And the little House Child said, 'The Butcher's boy gave me the bird; he said it wasn't a singer, but only a Reedbird.'

"'Singer or not,' said the man, 'it is a savage thing to wear. Suppose its mate were to see it now, how sorry he would feel. It may have lived in this very meadow. Do you think it is a good way to treat your guests?'

"Then the little girl felt very badly, and said that she 'didn't think.' It seems to me that that miserable Puk-Wudjie, Did-Not-Think, has a great deal of influence with House People.

"Then the man said, 'I know that you are sorry. Take the poor bird from your hat, and we will bury it here.' So they cut the threads that held her down and buried my mate in the meadow."

The Bobolink stopped a moment to take breath, and chancing to look at Tommy-Anne saw that she had her face in her hands, and Waddles was trying to lick away some tears that ran between her fingers.

"Why, what's the matter? are you sick?" cried Bob; "or perhaps you are sorry about my mate. It's very kind of you, I'm sure."

"No," said Tommy-Anne; "I'm not sick, but I *am* sorry. It was my hat your wife was sewed to. I never used to understand how birds and other animals felt, when I lived in the city. Of course I read about you all in books and knew in *words* that it is not nice to kill you, but somehow I did not *realize* you until I came here." And she seemed so grieved that Bob hastily continued his story to divert her.

"This that I have told you, Tommy-Anne, is the life of the birds that come and go. They leave at different times and go to various places in winter, each one following the law of his family, but for a jeering, jolly southern gentleman, you'll not fine *my* match in twenty counties. Did you say rice?"

"But how is it with the birds who stay here always?" asked Tommy-Anne.

"That story belongs to my friend Robin Thrush, who will sing after intermission; allow me to introduce him," said Robert of Lincoln, with a bow and a flourish.

"One moment, please," called the Song-Sparrow; "a song comes next. Miou, I think it is your turn."

V

MIOU'S SONG

AFTER the intermission, the birds returned to the old tree, gathering in little groups to chat, looking occasionally at the sun to calculate the time to evensong.

Ko-ko-ko-ho aroused himself sufficiently to look intelligent, and came quite to the edge of the wood to join his wife. Their three owlets were hatched in March, but, as they always grow slowly, were still in the nest. Ko-ko-ko-ho blinked several times on coming into brighter light, then dropped quickly to the ground, where he secured a luckless mouse. Ko-ko-ko-ho intended to eat the mouse himself, but the Missis said something to him, and he changed his mind and flew noiselessly with it into the deep woods to his nest.

"Suppose we follow him," said Tommy-Anne to Waddles. Returning early from their luncheon, they had been lying under the tree, talking to a couple of Puk-Wudjies, who had come out to locate a new village, in place of one that had been washed away the previous night.

"I don't know where Ko-ko-ko-ho lives, mistress," said Waddles. "I cannot follow the scent of a bird when it flies, you know. Perhaps one of the Puks can tell us."

"Certainly, certainly we will," they cried, in squeaky, mouse-like voices. "It is not so very far from here, — in the old wood, where the trees have never been cut, and the nest is in a hickory tree on the top of the great rock ledge. Ko-ko-ko-ho has chased away Ondaig, the Crow, and used the ruins of his nest to build his own upon. The way is very rough for us little vanishing people ; will you let us ride on your back, Mr. Waddles ?"

Without waiting for an answer, much to Waddles' surprise and disgust, they climbed hand over hand up his tail and seated themselves side by side on his back.

"Two can play at that game," said he, sitting down so suddenly that the Puks coasted off into the grass.

"I'm ashamed of you, Waddles," said Tommy-Anne; "let them ride."

"Where are you going?" the Song-Sparrow called. "The time is nearly up, and I hear Miou crossing the meadow."

"We were going to find Ko-ko-ko-ho's nest."

Mrs. Ko-ko-ko-ho laughed aloud, and all the other birds gave cautious exclamations of horror!

"Is it wrong to look at the nest?" said Tommy-Anne, glancing from one to the other, as if she was not sure which individual had the right to answer her.

"Not at all wrong," said Mrs. Ko-ko-ko-ho; "I'm perfectly willing that you should look *at* it or *in* it, either."

"For shame!" cried the birds, in chorus (overcoming the fear they felt of the Ko-ko-ko-hos, who frequently fed upon their smaller brethren). "Tommy-Anne, the BAD ONE lives in the ledge below the tree that holds their nest!"

They evidently expected that she would be terrified, but, not understanding what they meant, she asked, "What bad one?"

More murmurs of surprise, and then Thrasher, the great brown Mocking Thrush, who sings like a real Mockingbird, flew up, lashing his tail, and said : —

"Listen, Tommy-Anne; the BAD ONE is the

sly, ash-brown serpent who carries in his tail the noise of winds, who bears the pit mark of the criminal under his slit-shaped eyes, and wears the glanded death fangs in his jaws. The BAD ONE is CROTALUS—the RATTLESNAKE!"

Tommy-Anne started at this, for she once heard the Miller tell her father that she might safely go in all the woods, for there were none of these snakes anywhere about, not even on Wild Cat Mountain. The birds were now evidently satisfied that she was properly impressed, and Thrasher continued: —

"He alone of all his family remains in these

parts. His mate was killed a year ago by a strange hunter, and now he lives in solitude in the ledge of rocks where hundreds of his companions once found secret hiding-places in winter, or sunned themselves on the gray-mossed steps in summer."

" Why is not Ko-ko-ko-ho afraid of him? " said Tommy-Anne.

" Tell her, Mrs. Ko-ko-ko-ho," said Thrasher; but the Owl had disappeared. " I don't wonder she flew away," said Thrasher. " The truth is that Crotalus and Ko-ko-ko-ho have gone into partnership! "

" Partnership! how, pray ? "

" Crotalus is old, childless and discouraged, and dares not any longer hunt openly for himself, so Ko-ko-ko-ho has agreed to supply him with food as long as he lives, — mice, lizards, small birds, etc., — and Crotalus in return promised to protect the Owl's nest from enemies. So when the old Owls wish to leave the nest, Crotalus mounts guard at the foot of the tree."

" How I wish that I might safely see this Bad One!" sighed Tommy-Anne. " When he dies, the chance will be gone, and I want to see *everything*."

" Then you must ask Ko-ko-ko-ho; he is the only one who can promise you safety on the rocky ledge."

" Recess is over, gentlemen and ladies; come to

your places," called the Song-Sparrow, ushering Tommy-Anne back to her seat on the bough, kindly picking off a spider who was spreading his net across the back of it, and turning with a flourish to Miou, saying, "If he is ready, the Gray Prince of Garden Birds will give us a ballad."

Miou was quite ready to sing, and perching jauntily opposite Tommy-Anne, after bowing to her, ran the gamut on his pitch-pipe, and began in his best concert manner, using all the gestures for which he is famous.

I

> In the grapevine of your garden,
> I flirt and do my singing.
> Sing high!   Coquillico!   Coquillico!
> In the lilacs of your garden
> My quips and jests are ringing.
> Sing low!   Coquillico!   Coquillico!
> (I answer yes!   I answer no!
> I mimic, as they come and go,
> My neighbours.)
>
> In the nest that *we* made,
> On the eggs that *she* laid,
> Broods the Missis:
> Perky Missis!
> Spare a berry,
> Or a cherry,
> For my merry
> Merry Missis!

(We answer yes!   We answer no!
We gossip as they come and go
With neighbours.)

II

When the chipmunk's tail is jerking,
We're 'ware our nest of leaving.
Prut!   Prut!   Coquillico!   Coquillico!
In his thoughts there's danger lurking
Though his looks are quite deceiving.
Zay!   Zay!   Coquillico!   Coquillico!
(I sing you yes!   I scold you no!
I worry as they come and go,
My neighbours.)

From the nest that *we* made,
All the eggs that *she* laid
Would be missing.
While he chattered
Hopes be shattered,
Eggs be scattered,
Eggs be missing!
(We sing you yes!   We scold you no!
We watch you as you come and go
Like neighbours.)
And still from dawn till close of day,
Until winds whistle us away,
We'll sing to you and scold to you
Like neighbours.

As Miou ended, he flew to Tommy-Anne, gave
her a gentle caressing touch on the cheek with

H

his wing, and sped off in the direction of the garden. But though she clapped her hands, and all the birds shouted approval, the Song-Sparrow would not allow him to be recalled, because there were two songs and two stories yet to be heard.

VI

THE LEGEND OF OPECHEE

THE Robin's nest was in the apple tree, so that
he was near at hand when his name was called.
He had rather an awkward manner, and his speaking voice was harsh in comparison to his singing,
and he seemed embarrassed also at having to talk
to so large a company, and at a loss where to
begin.

Tommy-Anne quickly put him at his ease by
exclaiming: "You dear fat thing! I'm always
so glad to see you, for you are one of my cheerful birds, you know."

"Am I really," said the Robin, looking pleased;
"but what are your cheerful birds?" And all
the others seemed anxious to know.

Tommy-Anne, feeling rather shy at having to explain herself in company, hesitated a little and then said: "You see last winter was the first snow season that I had been here, and I was rather lonely, because I had not made all the friends that I have now. I saw strange birds in the trees and strange footprints in the snow, but before I could learn the birds' names they were gone, and the tracks in the snow were drifted over before I could follow them.

"But I knew you, Mr. Robin, and the Chickadee, the Song-Sparrow and the Bluebird, and after a little, I *guessed* the Goldfinch (though he had shed his yellow feathers), because he always flies the same way, with a little dip as if he meant to drop, and then jerks up again as if he had changed his mind at the last minute. So whenever I saw any one of you five darlings, I used to say: 'Brace up, Waddles; if those little birds can be cheerful outside there, without any fire, I think we can be cheerful too.'"

"I wasn't gloomy," protested Waddles; "there are lots of things to chase in winter, and the trails don't mix up as they do now, and you very seldom bothered me by following."

"Be quiet and don't interrupt, sir. So when father saw any of you in the evergreens, or pick-

ing up the seed we scattered for you at the door,
he always called, 'Come and look, little daughter;
here are some of your cheerful birds!'"

At this Mr. Robin grew very friendly and
spoke quite at his ease. "I'm a popular bird,"
he said, "though I could never understand exactly why."

"Neither could I," said the Thrasher, jealously.
"I'm much better looking and I have a stronger
voice and lots more style. Some things go by
contraries, and popularity is one of them."

"Order! order! I am surprised at you," said
the Song-Sparrow.

"I think in the beginning," continued the
Robin, placidly, "the reason the House People
liked me was because I was somehow confused
with my English relative Robin Redbreast, who
is famous in history for having so kindly fur-
nished a leaf quilt to the poor Babes in the
Wood; and who, later on, was the victim of the
tragedy whose anniversary we are celebrating.
Now my cousin Robin Redbreast had the advantage of me in personal beauty, as his children
have to this day, being smaller, sleeker, brighter
in colour, in shape more like Owaissa, the Bluebird.

"I have tried to look up the early history of

our family, but like many such things the records may be read in several ways, and I am indebted to Wawa, whose ancestors were present in great numbers at the time, for the following information.

"The Red Brothers were fond of us, holding us birds of love and good omen, and they protected us, giving us the name of *Opechee*. When the first House People came to these parts after their hardships on the rocky shore and barren beaches, they found us here in vast flocks, and seeing that we were confiding and that our breast colour was somewhat like, they called us Robin, after the Robin Redbreast of their home gardens.

" Another reason for my popularity is, that while I am not very clever, or quick to see things, I am good-tempered, and never, even under the greatest temptation, suck eggs, or show resentment if other birds build near my nest. And as I appear a trifle stupid, very little is expected of me, and so when I sing my best, every one marvels.

" Finally, I am not particular about my food. Of course I *prefer* nice juicy worms and bugs, with a fruit dessert, but I can live on almost anything, keeping up a brave heart in winter, on a frugal dish of frozen honeysuckle berries. Thus some members of my family are with you at all seasons, when most of the Song Birds have been forced away by hunger ; so it is true that we are one of those that the House Child calls 'the cheerful birds,' one of the few who, nesting nearby, linger to give some scraps of summer melody to cheerless days.

"My grandparents were an old-fashioned, stay-at-home couple. They lived down in the village, in the Parson's garden. This garden has always been thought a very comfortable home for our family, and especially so when the old man and his daughter lived there.

"When his neighbours said, 'Why not set traps or spread nets to catch the birds that eat your fruit,' he answered, 'These birds work with me in the garden, keeping away the slug and worm, while their sweet music gladdens my heart; why should they not have wages? Let them take their tithes.'"

"Were you with the flock that sat all huddled together in the pines, the day in March, when the last snow fell and the sun melted it away in an hour ?" asked Tommy-Anne.

"Yes, that was our flock ; we were all strong, newly moulted males, some old, some the young of last year. For several months we had been living many miles west of here, in the great evergreen swamps, with the flocks of crested Cedar-birds and Blue Jays.

"Shawondasee came creeping into our retreat, saying: 'Gheezis turns in his course to-day and faces summerward. I go northward to prepare a garden; will you not keep me company?'

"So we followed him; but when we reached this orchard after our long flight, our hearts grew heavy, for Peboan was still here, and his breath hung heavily on everything, so we huddled in the pines for shelter, chiding Shawondasee for deceiving us. But he answered only one word— *Wait!*

"While we waited, you came out, and that House Fourfoot, Waddles, ran before you, showing you where we were hidden. This made us sadder yet, for we said, 'If Fourfoot can see us so easily in the pines, how can we hope to hide ourselves in nesting-time?'

"Then Gheezis pushed through the clouds, putting Kabibonokka to flight, loosened Peboan's grasp, and we began calling to each other, while Owaissa, the Bluebird, peeped into his house box under the eaves to see if all was in order for the few straws he calls his nest. After that our anxious season came quickly. We are often very unfortunate with our nests. They are made of

sticks and grass plastered and lined with clay,
you know, the commonest kind that you see.
For some strange reason we have partly forgotten the law that Heart of Nature gave us for
the hiding of our nests, or the exact spot where it
is best to place them. So you will find them
everywhere, in bushes near the ground, and in
tall treetops.

"This year I have had very poor luck," sighed
the Robin. "My mate is a young bird, and it was
her first experience in housekeeping. Her family
lived in the Miller's grape arbour, so to please her
we located our first nest there. We were rather
hurried in building, owing to some heavy rain-
storms, and we did not realize, until the nest was
done and one green-blue egg laid, that we had
chosen an open place where no vine leaves would
grow to shelter our young.

"That same afternoon, as I was returning home,
I chanced to look ahead. There, stalking through
the grass toward the nest, was Tiger, the Miller's
cat! To me she seemed as big and savage as
Rufus Lynx, the mountain wild cat."

("I quite agree with you," growled Waddles,
under his breath.)

"He lashed his tail and lifted his paws so carefully that the grass did not even suspect his com-

ing, then crouched to spring. For a wonder I called, 'Quick! quick!' at the right moment, and my mate immediately flew to me without looking behind her. At the same time Tiger made a leap, dragging the nest to the ground and breaking the egg.

"We next tried your garden, for Johnny Wren told us that the House People who lived there did not keep cats, but only a bandy-legged Fourfoot, who was so short and fat that he could not reach up far, even to *look* into a nest."

"Who? What?" barked Waddles, jumping up, "Did Johnny Wren say that? We won't let him perch on our clothes poles to sing, any more, will we, mistress?"

"I didn't mention names," the Robin hastened to say, "though if ever you look at yourself in the pond, you must see that you are both bandy and *very* fat!" And then the Robin could not understand why he had only made matters worse by the explanation.

"We built the second nest on the end of a well-protected pine branch. That night a soaking rain drenched it through and through, making it into a mud pie. The branch was too slender, and the wet nest weighed it down, and then dropped to the ground. Now we have a firm lodging in this tree, and to-morrow our four eggs will be birds, we hope. My wife has been very anxious all day on account of the noise of the anniversary, but I said, 'Stay still, my dear, and keep your temper, and I will attend to everything.' You can see the tip of her beak and the end of her tail from here, if you look up."

" How lovely ! " said Tommy-Anne. " May I come to-morrow and see your children hop out of the eggs? "

" You *could* come, of course, but I would much prefer that you should wait a bit. Our children do not hop out of the eggs ; they are quite top-heavy and helpless, — all eyes and mouth. It makes us very nervous, clearing away the shells and all that, without having any one to watch us. I'm afraid if you came you might make us upset ourselves again."

" What do your children look like when they are young? Are they all soft and downy like my little chickens and ducklings? "

"Oh no, Tommy-Anne; our young are naked, and their great round eyes are tightly closed, and it is several weeks before they are fully feathered and fit to fly."

"How very funny! I saw some little Sea Gulls last summer, when we were at the shore, and father took me sailing to the great island; and they could walk down to the water's edge and find food as soon as they were hatched. In fact, the eggs lay on the sand without hardly any nest for the poor things to stay in if they wished."

"Heart of Nature has arranged it so that the

birds whose parents build poor nests, or none at all, gain the feathers in the egg, but those of us who belong to the Brotherhood of Builders are able to give our young warm lodgings, so they are hatched naked and helpless, and gain their strength and feathers in the nest."

"What is the Brotherhood of Builders?" asked Tommy-Anne.

"The history of it is the Oriole's story, and I have not finished my own yet. To-morrow when those eggs are hatched I shall be able to go to my club, and in a few days all the members will have gathered again."

"Your club? Do birds have clubs?"

"Certainly they do. Our club house is in the belt of old cedar trees between your house and the road."

"Why do you go there when the little birds are hatched? I should think you would have to stay at home and help feed them."

"I do stay at home all day, but mother Robins always insist upon putting their babies to sleep themselves; they say we men are in the way. Then we meet together, the males of each community, or flock, by themselves, and choosing some thick trees for shelter, we make a musical club, gathering at dusk to sing our evensong, and breaking up after matins, each one returning to his family.

"By and by when the first brood leave the nest, we take them to roost with us at the club, leaving their mothers free to tend the second brood, and when the nesting is over, we all rove together in great flocks, keeping away until the summer moult is over, but coming to your lawn again before the Moon of Falling Leaves."

"Please, what family do you belong to?"

"We are of the Silver-tongued, — the family of Thrushes."

"Thrushes? You do not look like the other Thrushes that I know," said Tommy-Anne. "The Wood Thrush that sings every afternoon, beyond the garden, has a brown back and a speckled breast, and the Echo Thrush, in the river woods, is tawny on the back and is marked with little arrow spots under his chin. Your back is dark, and your breast is the same colour as flower pots, and then you sing differently too. Every Robin has a song of his own, but the Thrushes have each one tune that they all keep repeating."

"It is true that our colour is different from our brothers, but so is that of Owaissa, who is also of our family. We sing strange songs, truly, each one telling his story in his own words, and no one of the House People understanding it, or you would know why our breasts are ruddy and have lost their spots. The reason of this lies in the farback, and even the legend of it is so old that the wisest of the White-headed Eagles, who told it to me, did not know when it first was shaped to words."

"Please tell us the legend," urged Tommy-Anne, glancing appealingly toward the Song-Sparrow, who, seeing that Gheezis was looking at the earth slantwise, said: "There really is not time — unless perhaps the Kingbird would be willing to wait and tell his story when the birds of the air meet for their flying practice."

"I would much rather wait," replied the King-bird, "for then I shall have more to tell. Beside, I'm belated now, my nest is not finished, and it must be done to-night, as I have promised several friends to chase Crows for them to-morrow morning."

"Chase Crows? What have the Crows been doing?"

"The same as usual, the cowards! Sneaking into Robins' nests and sucking the eggs, stealing a young bird here, another there. But it was not for nothing that the Red Brothers called me the *Sachem*. Ondaig flies in terror, covering his eyes as best he may, when two or three of us are abroad. You too, friend Tchin, you are not above bird-nesting." And he made a rapid pass at the Blue Jay, who screamed with surprise.

"Now you will have plenty of time for your story," said Tommy-Anne to the Robin, dropping from her branch to the ground.

"Once upon a time —" began the Robin.

Tommy-Anne chuckled contentedly, pulling Waddles over, until his head rested upon her lap. "All nice comfortable stories begin 'Once upon a time,'" she said.

"Once upon a time," continued the Robin, not heeding the interruption, "before the old trees had been cut in the forests, and the wild animals roamed among them ; when the Panther, the Wolf, and the Moose were in plenty, and the great Black Bears picked the wild-grape clusters, and robbed A-moe, the Honey Bee, of the packages of sweets that he had hidden in tree hollows ; before the House People came over the salt water to teach the Red Brothers to break faith with Heart of Nature, and kill the Wild Wood Brethren for other purposes than food and covering ; on the top of Wild Cat Mountain, in his skin-covered wigwam, lived Kaniwa, the Chief of his tribe, and his only child Wenonah.

The timorous Gray Rabbits came forth in the moonlight. —p. 115.

114

" Wenonah had grown up in this place alone with her father; for her mother had disappeared one spring night when Wenonah was a babe. Stolen by wild beasts some thought, but others shook their heads, saying that she was the daughter of Weeng, the Spirit of Sleep, who had come before day-dawn and carried her away; but from that day Kaniwa's wigwam was lonely.

" Wenonah left the wigwam reluctantly and returned eagerly. She loved Heart of Nature and the things he ruled, more than those things belonging to the third ruler, Heart of Man."

(" Heart of Man ! that means people ; now I know another *why*," whispered Tommy-Anne to herself.)

" The beasts all loved Wenonah. The Wild Cat smoothed his snarl into a smile, and carried his furry cubs in his mouth to her that she might caress them. The shiest Moose would kneel before her to have his head rubbed. Chetowaik, the Plover, every season brought for her eating some of his most treasured eggs ; Subbe-ka-she, the Spider, wove rare lace for her ; and Shi-sheeb, the painted Wood Duck, moulted his gayest feathers for her decking. The timorous Gray Rabbits come forth in the moonlight, circling about her and doing their dances and jumping tricks to please her ; while even the Bad One crept silent and abashed from her path. So the old women wagged their heads again and said, 'She is like her mother and not of us, some night she will vanish, before she is grown a woman.'

"Of all living things, she loved the birds the best, and among them we came first, and next to us the Bluebirds. In the Moon of Leaves we both flocked near her, as she pulled the blossoms from the wild plum trees, or sought the pink and white Miskodeed (the flower you call spring beauty) in the meadow.

"In Moon of Strawberries we followed her through all the woods as she made flower-gar-lands and, giving them messages to her vanished mother, threw them in the swift river.

"In Moon of Falling Leaves, when the women ground samp, pounding it in a rock-bowl hollowed on the cliff, we would surround her, lest unawares she moved too near the edge.

"Early one summer, trouble entered Kaniwa's heart. At noon, when he used to go abroad, the old warrior sat at home, counting the notches of his time-stick, an anxious look upon his face."

"Please, what is a 'time-stick?'" asked Tommy-Anne.

" The Red Brothers counted the time by notches on a stick, one cut for each snow season. When twenty were cut, they laid the stick away and began another, as in Birdland we count by the nesting seasons.

" Wenonah saw that her father was sad, but she kept on singing to A-moe and his work-people, who were buzzing about the fragrant wild-grape flowers. When she raised her voice, the bees flew away in alarm, but when she dropped it to a murmuring like to their own speech, they crowded about her, and the words that she sang were these : —

> " The poor little bee
> That lives in the tree,
> The poor little bee
> That lives in the tree,
> Has but one arrow in his quiver ![1]

" ' Fifteen snows have gone,' muttered the warrior ; ' what if the old wives say truly, and my child should leave me ? '

" Wenonah heard the words and started, a wild look coming into her eyes, but she quickly grew calm and laughed merrily to comfort him.

" ' Why do you laugh, my daughter ? '

[1] Kaniga nursery rhyme.

"'I laugh with my brother, Shawondasee, the South Wind,' said Wenonah, letting her long black hair float out on his breath as he hurried past.

"But when the Moon of Snow-Shoes came again, and Kaniwa cut a new notch ou his stick, the sixteenth since her birth, he grew anxious, and once more. she laughed wildly, stroking her tent companion, a Gray Squirrel, and answering her father gaily, 'I laugh at Mahng, the Loon ; do you not hear him wailing down by the watercourse?'

"Still, again, her father was satisfied ; but when Segwun, the Spring, gladdened the land, Wenonah gathered us the closer, stroked our feathers, whispering, 'Do not fail me, dear brothers ! Little brothers, you will not fail me?' And though not knowing what she meant, we promised.

"One night when we were roosting in the trees, a shadow came among us. It was Wenonah, and she called, 'Brothers ! Brothers! The time has come ! I need you. Wait by the wigwam when the darkness thins, at the hour when night and morning wrestle for the owning of the heavens ; and be silent !'

"So we gathered noiselessly, as the night went on. Wawonaissa, the Whip-poor-will, cried, and then ceased, and long the Marsh Frogs peeped, before a glow spread upward from the earth's edge to where the Morning Star blazed.

"Out from the tent curtains stepped Wenonah, her filmy garments hanging about her like the petals of the wind-flower, but her face shone like the Star she gazed at. We were frightened, but she spoke lightly to us: 'I go to my mother beyond the Morning Star; come thou part way with me, that my flight may be unseen.'

"Stooping, she took some earth and rubbed a little on the breast of each one of us, saying: 'This is in token that you shall return again in safety to earth.' With that, she stepped from the cliff, Shawondasee bearing her aloft, as our wings bear us, and surrounding her we flew eastward.

"Always it grew lighter, and we felt the breath of Gheezis hot upon our breasts, and the moist earth upon them burned red in colour like brick-clay. Seeing this, Wenonah, turning, said, 'You must leave me now, returning earthward.'

"'No, we will follow you,' we cried, all the warm-hearted Bluebirds beginning to weep sadly.

"'You may not follow where I go, for the speech of that country is unknown to you. Return, my brothers!'

"'A token! give us a token!' we cried.

"Still looking at us, she saw the reddening of our breasts, and said, 'Forget your stripes and spots, my Robins, and wear forever on your faithful breasts the earth-colour, reddened in my service by the touch of morning!

"'And you, my Bluebirds, sweethearts, carry on your shoulders the blue sky of my new home to be the spring sign of your Earth Mother.' And she gently rubbed the rusty edges from their feathers until they were bright blue.

"Once more she said, 'Return, my brothers,' and then we no longer saw her, and we obeyed.

"When we reached the mountain, it was full morning, and there was a sound of weeping about the wigwam, and within lay a shape they called Wenonah, and they said, 'She is dead!'

"But we knew better.

"To this day we have kept our ruddy breasts, and Owaissa his blue back and sad note; and if our young show, at first, some of the old-time stripes, they quickly moult away."

When the Robin ended, all the birds remained silent and seemed deeply impressed. But the story of his ancestors did not trouble Mr. Robin or make him sad, and after giving his listeners a little bobbing bow, he was soon on the ground, trying to jerk out an earthworm, that was twice

his own length, and held itself down as firmly as
if possessed of six feet and a dozen pairs of hands,
and the Song-Sparrow called upon the Oriole for
his story.

VII

THE BROTHERHOOD OF BUILDERS

"Here I am, B. Oriole, at your service," called the beauty, hanging to the branch like a bit of richly coloured tropic fruit, and burying his black head in a flower cluster, while he skilfully took up a collection of insects, turning so that his orange feathers flashed like flame.

"What does B. stand for?" asked Tommy-Anne.

"B. stands for Baltimore, my first name. I have to use the letter to distinguish myself from my brother, O. (orchard) Oriole, who wears darker feathers, and who *was* supposed to live mostly in orchards."

"Did you come from Baltimore?"

"No indeed, we are from the country; but that city and we birds both took our name from the same person. Long ago when there were few House People in this land, a very up-top House Person came sailing into the waters near some woods where thousands of us lived. (That was before the days when these same House People made war upon us and nearly turned our whole family into bonnet trimmings for their women.) He admired us so much, that he chose our colours for his totem, and in return gave us his very best name, which was Baltimore, Baron Baltimore. But as Birdland is a Republic, of course we left off the Baron and contented ourselves with plain Baltimore."

"Cock-a-doodle-doo!" screamed a rooster, far away on the barnyard wall.

"Yankee-Doodle, you hear, is responding to my patriotic sentiments. Not only are we all equal in Birdland, but, with a few exceptions, we are all workers, and our motto is,—Scratch or starve, fly or freeze." (Applause and cheering from the small birds.)

"Are you really equals?" asked Tommy-Anne, in astonishment. "I should think that a poor little Wren was the *unequal* of Ko-ko-ko-ho or a great Hawk."

"So he would be in a square out-of-cover fight, but Heart of Nature arranges matters so that the Wren not only has plenty of places to hide, but also two or three times as many children every year, as either the Owl or the Hawk ; so that numbers make up for size, and dodging for strength."

" Who rules in Birdland ? "

" We have no visible ruler, but the laws are put in our hearts."

" Somebody must have made the laws."

" Certainly, the First Heart made the Plan, and Heart of Nature sees that it is carried out."

" Suppose that you don't choose to obey ? "

" Then we always suffer, and usually die."

" Why is not Heart of Nature King then ? "

" Because he created nothing, and has no power of himself ; he only directs."

"I don't think that Birdland is a bit of a Republic ; I call it an ' off-with-your-head Monarchy,'" said Tommy-Anne, whose idea of kings was based on the death-dealing powers of Henry VIII. and his daughter Mary.

" And I say it is a *Republic*," cried B. Oriole ; " because we all lose our heads *equally*, — Hawk and Wren alike ! "   He had become quite excited, and his voice seemed to come through the top of his head ; but he soon grew calm again, and continued : —

"In Birdland we are interested in science, music, agriculture, and art. Bug-hunting is our science ; you House People give it another name, — e-n-t-o-m-o-l-o-g-y, I think. We express our music chiefly by singing and whistling, though we have some good pipers among us, and the Ruffed Grouse and all of our Woodpeckers are expert drummers. We are farmers also, both sowing and reaping, for we gather fruits and various seeds for food, and we are also the sowers of them in our flights and migrations, while the waste of our bodies fertilizes the ground where they fall, making barren places bloom.

"Our trade is house-building; and this is why our chief society is called The Brotherhood of Builders.

"When we rove in flocks all through the late summer and autumn, or frolic in our winter picnic-grounds in the south, needing no homes, we camp out. Any tree is good enough for a bachelor's perch. But when we gather in our summer haunts, we must have some sort of basket ready to hold the eggs that are always laid at this season, and this basket must also serve as a house for the young, until they are ready to care for themselves ; so for this we build nests."

"I know all about that; but why do you have so many kinds of nests? Why do you always lay eggs at this time of year?"

The Oriole did not like to be so constantly interrupted, and stopped short, being really quite offended, and had to be coaxed by the Song-Sparrow, and receive an apology from Tommy-Anne before he would proceed.

Finally he said, "Why are not all birds of the same size and colour? Why don't we all sing the same song? Every one of us is suited to the place and way in which he is intended to live, and the same rule follows in regard to our nests.

"We well understand the art of making the nest, in its general colour, like the surroundings in which it must be placed. As these are different, so must the nests be unlike. The reason that we are made to lay our eggs in the spring and early summer is, that food is then the most abundant, and there is plenty of time before cold weather for the birdlings to grow.

"As there must be many differently shaped nests, so it takes many materials to make them, and the materials must be put together in various ways. To do this, Heart of Nature has taught us the trades best suited to the work, and this knowledge has become an inheritance, so that we know by instinct how and where and when to build.

"The smaller, dull-coloured birds blend themselves and their nests with the grass, earth browns, and leafage of low bushes. The brightly coloured, like the Tanager, and myself, choose high trees. The larger ones, like Ko-ko-ko-ho, build in dark woods where dead limbs and litter conceal them, and so on all through Birdland.

"Heart of Nature has also arranged that we shall live near our work."

"Near your work? what work do *you* do?" said Tommy-Anne, forgetting herself again.

"Our work is the same as the House People's, — scratching and hopping about all day, to fill the stomachs of ourselves and families, and try to make them contented," said B. Oriole, in a tone which implied that he considered Tommy-Anne very stupid. "Of course we have the advantage over you in the matter of clothes, for as ours grow on, we are never bothered with shopping, and are always sure of a good fit. Consequently, I mean that we try to place our nests as near to our feeding-places as possible. This living near the feeding-grounds is what makes some water-birds have nothing but Humpty-Dumpty nests."

“Humpty-Dumpty nests!”

“Yes; that is, no nest at all. Don’t you know Humpty Dumpty who sat on the wall?

I thought that was a song which the House People made. Humpty Dumpty was an egg, you know, that fell off the wall where it was laid; *we* always thought that it must have been a Nighthawk’s egg, because they lay them on rocks and such places.

“The first thing we do after we have selected a mate, is to choose the nesting place.”

“Why don’t you build the nest first, and have it ready for a surprise for your mate?”

“Hoighty toighty!” ejaculated the Oriole, nearly falling off the bough in surprise. “House Child, when were you hatched? Are you a this spring's bird? You are evidently much younger than you look !

"Choose a site and build a nest without consulting the missis? I wonder at you! No, my dear, in Birdland the missis not only very often insists upon building the nest herself, but is *very* particular about the lumber her husband brings for the work, and he is lucky if she does not throw half of it away. Mrs. B. Oriole always does the building, and only last week I took her a lovely bunch of long red silk floss, and she said — but I will tell you that later; I'm wandering, and must go back to my story of the Brotherhood.

"We number in this trades-union of ours, carpenters, masons, weavers, basket-makers, tent-makers, felters, and decorators of many kinds; half of us work at several of these trades, and we are all upholsterers.

"As you might expect, the carpenters have the strongest homes, those the most resembling your houses, for they have a roof, sides, and a doorway. Instead of troubling to build up a house in a manner needing many tools, they bore theirs out, using only one tool, a combination of chisel and hammer, which they always carry with them."

"I wonder what bird it can be. Please tell

K

me its name; I can understand so much better when I know a person's name."

"Think a minute, Tommy-Anne. What rather large birds find their food by walking about trees, and pecking and hammering at the bark?"

"Woodpeckers, to be sure; but you said these carpenter birds lived in houses, with roofs and all that, and Woodpeckers live in nothing but a hole."

"Has not a hole a roof and sides? and how do they get in except through the doorway?"

"To be sure," answered Tommy-Anne, somewhat disappointed, "but where is the hammer and chisel, and how do they use them?"

"The chisel is the bill with which they chip away the softened wood (they always begin the hole in a partly decayed spot), and the hammer is the bird's head which drives the bill.

"You must remember, however, that every bird who has a nest in a hole is not by any means a carpenter. Other birds take possession of the empty holes, that have been used in past seasons, and putting a few straws or feathers in them, use them as their homes. The Bluebird does this, and the Nuthatch with the white vest, and your 'cheerful bird' the Chicadee.

"The best masons we have among us here are

the Swallows, though many other brothers use wet clay to line their homes, or to plaster the twigs together, but the Barn Swallows, who build on the hayloft rafters, make a mud bracket, using their wide beaks for a trowel. Their cousins, the Eaves Swallows, make mud balls and plaster them together into long pocket nests which are fastened under sloping roof edges. Here, too, you see they are near their feeding-ground, which is the air.

"You could not count our basket-makers, or even remember their names if I should tell them. All stick and grass nests that have no special shape may be called baskets, though among them there are those who weave so evenly that they deserve separate attention.

"My sister O. Oriole is one of these. She holds a strand of grass with her beak for a needle, and darns to and fro around the twigs of a branch end, until she has made as neat a bit of basket-work as any one could with hands.

"The ground-built nests and those in bushes," continued the Oriole, "do not require to be as skilfully made as those in high trees where the wind sweeps. Of course we have clumsy workers in the union, the one law being that a member shall make a nest that will keep his eggs and young safe and comfortable ; but if they grow too shiftless and the eggs roll out, then we drop the bird from our membership.”

“ Have you had to drop many ? ”

“ Only a few, and that was because we were rather careless in admitting them in the beginning. The Nighthawk seldom made much of a nest, putting his eggs in a mossy rock hollow. We hoped that he might improve, but instead, one day the Barn Swallow saw some of these eggs lying on the tin roof of a village house. That was too much for us, and we expelled him. And the Whip-poor-will, his cousin, who is almost as heedless, was angry about the matter and resigned.

“ The Mourning Doves also made such poor nests that the eggs showed through the cracks and sometimes fell down, and so we dropped them.”

“ Are hens in the union? ”

“ Certainly not; they often lay on the bare earth, — at best they only turn round and round in the grass or a heap of hay or leaves, until they have made a hollow.”

“ To be sure ; and even Waddles, who is not a bird, can do that. He made so many of such nests in the Miller’s long grass last summer, that Aunt

Prue said we ought to pay the damages. But one day the man at the store gave me a lot of left-over eggs 'to have some fun with,' he said ; so I put two or three in each of Wad-dles' nests, to see if any hens would come and try to hatch them.

"The Miller came out and said he wondered what kink all the hens in the neighbour-hood had taken, to come and lay in his field. So he took the eggs home and set them under his cross brown hen, but only two hatched. One was a duck and the other a white rooster ! The duck disap-peared, but the rooster grew up."

"I know where the duck went," said a Night-hawk, who had come out extra early to catch moths for supper, dropping so suddenly that the air rushed through his white spotted wings with a booming noise, and then turning upward again at the moment when you expected he would strike the ground.

"I think that it is *mean* to tell tales," said Waddles, looking up reproachfully. "When I didn't enjoy that duck one bit either, for I swallowed it too fast, and I had a dreadful pain all night, and had to eat sharp grass for three days for medicine."

"Who told the tale, you or I? Guilty conscience! I think the Whip-poor-will must be in the vicinity," said the Nighthawk, screaming with laughter, in which all the birds joined.

B. Oriole said: "I must hurry, for it is truly late when the Nighthawk begins his evening meal, but I will tell you about three weavers before I go.

"The first is Ruby-throat, the messenger of the Flower Market. The second is *Sweet*, the Yellow Warbler with the streaked breast, who lives in your orchard, and the third is myself, or rather Mrs. B. O., my better half, who has to-day finished our home in the great elm that hangs over your house, Tommy-Anne."

"I thought that you were building up there," she replied; "I almost fell out of the attic window trying to look at you; but whichever way I turned, a branch or twig came in the way. And when I looked up from the ground, my head nearly fell off backwards."

"That shows how carefully our twig was chosen, though I can't say that I gave one word of advice concerning it.

"To begin with Mrs. Ruby-throat's nest; as you know, who have seen her, she is here, there, and everywhere. She begins at dawn down in the shade, stripping the strong young ferns of their woolly coverings; next out in the sun, chasing the fleeting dandelion down ; then up to some slender branch of beech, elm, or maple, where she sets her collection of fluff saddle-wise and commences to compact it and fasten it down with what? — A little cord of cobweb.

"Round and round she twines this, then is off again. When all is fastened firmly, and the tiny cup well rounded, she brings other gear in her beak — the coloured lichen scales that cling to old trees and rocks ; these she fastens with mouth-glue to the outside of the nest, covering its rounded edge completely with the frescoing, until it would take the eye of a Kingbird to separate it from the branch it rests upon.

"Thus her home is hidden from beast, bird, and House People, and as she darts to it, who can follow?

"The wind, perchance, the sun-ray that plays upon Mr. Ruby-throat's jewelled collar; the dragon fly, or the spider looking for a frame wherein to spread his net for fly-fishing.

"If a feathered brother comes too near, — beware! Sir Ruby-throat carries a rapier! The messenger of the Flower Market goes well armed, and fights fierce battles in defence of the news he carries, and little cares he if he runs this sword in a too inquisitive eye.

"The Yellow Warbler, whom we call *Sweet*, because it is the chief word of his song, collects the threads for his weaving in plain sight. He, too, robs the ferns of their wool, but he also cleans your house boards of cobwebs, gleans horsehair, and shreds plant fibres into twine for lashing his findings to the forked apple twig or elderbush stalk.

"When he wishes down for lining, he does not chase through the air for it, but hopping along the ground, quickly pulls open the scarcely ripe seed-cases of the dandelions, getting a whole mouthful at once, with which he soon finishes his upholstery ; then spends his days singing 'sweet, sweet, sweeter ! ' and snatching soft chrysalids from the weather cracks to feed his missis.

" To my own nest at last. The brothers will not think me vain, I know, if I say that for safety and strength, neat workmanship, and skilful placing, it is the best, if not the prettiest, nest in Birdland.

" We male Orioles are gaily coloured, as you see. The eyes of House People and birds follow in our wake, but often it is the eye of envy and covetousness. In feeding we can scarcely hide ourselves in the thick leafage. What could we do, then, when added to our bright feathers the clamouring of our nestlings calls double attention to us ? for they are as noisy a brood as ever left the egg, clamouring for food, then clamouring because they have been fed. Heart of Nature says : 'Build high on the end of a supple branch, where beasts may not climb. Build a deep pocket nest, small at the top, so that from above as from below no eye may see therein.

" 'Make the nest strong, and hang it to the branch, so that it may yield to the wind, as the branch and its leaves yield, bending, but not breaking, and let there also be a leaf spray above to scatter the rain as it falls.'

"Then Heart of Nature says : 'Mind what you build *with;* the nest must be woven closely. Tread your flax from milkweed stalks and other tough fibres, and threads of bark, binding with hair, weaving in and out with claw and bill. Make the bottom thicker than the sides, bedding it well with hair or moss. Also let the female see to the weaving, for it needs the surety and cunning of her fashioning.'

"So from the beginning, in our family, the missis was the weaver. After many centuries, — when House People covered the land and kept the Hawks at bay, — when we built in friendly gardens, we made our nests less deep and larger at the top; but even now, if we build in wild lonely places, we make a long pouch and draw its mouth so closely that we may but slip in and out. This is the reason why our nests are found of many different shapes and sizes.

" With the coming of the House People we also varied our materials somewhat."

" Oh yes," said Tommy-Anne, "you were to tell us about the bunch of red floss that you brought home, and what your wife said about it."

" That wretched floss was a bit of trap string !

" Up at your house, one day, a woman sat weaving bright threads in a bit of ground that she held in her lap. As she worked, gay flowers grew up, following her needle through the ground.

" I said to myself, ' I should like some of that bright string to take home for the nest-making,' and at that moment the wind blew a tuft of it my way, and catching it in my beak, I flew to the elm."

" Do you always build in elms ? "

" Not always ; but we like them, because even the little twigs are so strong and never snap.

" As I was saying, I took the coloured floss home and offered it to the missis. She said, ' I don't like that stuff ; it is not smoothly twisted, the quality is poor, and I don't think it will wash,' and then she turned her back on it. I was disappointed and, man-like, judging by the looks, urged her to try a bit, dropping it where her claw clung to her weaving.

"She moved, and her claw caught on the soft stuff, caught aud would not let go.

" 'A trap, a trap!' she screamed, and into the bunch went her other claw and one of mine also, which I had stretched out to help her, and off the branch we fell, fluttering and struggling, each moment becoming more tangled together, until we reached the ground ; many neighbours following and vainly trying to help us.

" My wife cried, 'See what you have done ! We are as good as dead, if a cat or that House Four-foot sees us.' "

" Waddles would not have touched you," said Tommy-Anne, turning indignantly toward him ; " would you, sir ? "

" I wouldn't have *bitten*, mistress, but I might have sniffed and licked a little."

" By that time, we were in a hopeless tangle, wings and all, and lay quite still, panting.   A House Boy came along whistling, with a basket tipped over his head.   He saw us.   'This is worse than cats,' I said, 'for we shall be shut up in cages, like the poor Goldfinch, who only escaped to die, when he was sick and summer over.'

" The boy picked us up and unwound my wife

Let's shake hands. — p. 143.

first, but instead of letting her go, he put her under the basket, which he held down with his foot. I was in despair.

"Next the boy untangled me, and put me under the basket also. I fought and bit his finger ; but it was no use, under I went. In a minute he called, 'One, two, three, fly!' and lifted the basket. We flew!"

"It was the Butcher's boy! He always liked birds in cages, and now father and I try to make him see how much nicer they are in the trees, and he is learning, because he set you free. I remember now, he told me the other day that he found 'two Tom-fool Orioles' wound up in a skein of silk."

"That is true; we were Tom-fools, or rather *I* was."

"You must excuse his language for a while. Father says that it is no use in trying to make him understand about not saying some words until his mind becomes more civilized, and then he will know of himself."

"I think he is a *very* nice boy," said B. Oriole.

"So do I," answered Tommy-Anne, heartily; "let's shake hands. Oh! I forgot you haven't any; never mind, claw my finger instead, — so."

"The nest is done," said the Oriole, "and so is

my story; but I am afraid I shall never hear the last of that floss."

"Your own song now, brother Oriole; you were to sing," called the Song-Sparrow, "and then the anniversary will be over. Will you give us your bugle song?"

The Oriole swung himself on a hanging branch that rocked gently and began in a ringing voice, then ending very softly, vanished among the boughs where his mate waited by the nest.

"The anniversary is over," called the Song-Sparrow.

"Who is the champion singer of the year?" asked Tommy-Anne.

"You are the guest; you may decide," said all the birds, glad to avoid the responsibility.

"How can I?" said she; "they all sang best in their own way, and I love them all! What shall I say? But if I *must* choose, let it be Miou, because if he did not sing we should miss him so much in the garden."

"The Oriole made me feel very sleepy," said Waddles, yawning.

Then there was a good deal of fuss and bustle, and the birds said good-night and went their different ways.

Tommy-Anne and Waddles walked home. At

the gate she met her father and mother, who said together, "We have a piece of good news for you, little daughter."

"Oh, what can it be!" she cried, hugging them both at once, so that three heads bumped together.

Her father answered, "Shall I give you three guesses, or tell you at once?

"At once? then, — the Butcher is to let his boy come here every day through the summer to help your mother with her flowers, and I am to teach him his lessons at noon, so that he will be ready to go to school this winter. His father says he is 'daft to be a natural feller,' and has given his consent at last that he shall study."

"Naturalist, he means. Oh, how lovely!" Tommy-Anne cried, clapping her hands, and seizing Waddles by the fore paws and waltzing him about. "Then he can make the Rabbit pen, and hang the swing, and show me where the Wood Duck's nest is, and — "

"My dear," said her father, "I said that he was coming to help your *mother* with her *flowers*."

"Yes, yes, of course, father dear, but he can do the other things in the betweenties; you know he always makes *lots* of betweenties in a day " — a fact which Tommy-Anne's father knew only too well.

L

"What about Lac and Lactina?" said Tommy-Anne suddenly to Waddles. "That boy will leave birds alone, but how *can* I explain so that he will keep his feet off my snakes?" And Waddles agreed that the matter seemed difficult.

VIII

UNDERGROUND

Waddles was ill. He had a cold, and his stomach was so upset that he could not bear even the thought of his favourite breakfast of liver and bacon. Though it was a warm day, he shivered, snuffled, and spread himself out flat on the floor like a door mat.

"Poor dear, your nose is hot and as dry as bread crust, and you are dreadfully slobbery; we must have the Blacksmith," said Tommy-Anne, who found that all her attempts at petting met with no response other than a feeble tail-wag.

The Blacksmith, who was doctor to all the horses, cows, and dogs thereabout, looked at Waddles' eyes, felt his paw, and said, "He has the distemper" (which is a sort of whooping cough that most dogs have when they are children);

"beside that, he is much too fat; he must take physic, and stay in the woodshed and keep dry and quiet for a few days."

Waddles looked at his mistress appealingly; moving gave him such a headache that he felt willing to go to bed anywhere; yet he made up his mind that he would *not* take the medicine.

The physic that the Blacksmith mixed was dark brown and very sticky. Tommy-Anne insisted upon administering it herself, while the Butcher's boy held the invalid's head; but after the dose was poured down, there was much more of it on Waddles' nose and ears than in his little inside.

"I told you so," thought Waddles.

"Poof!" said the Butcher's boy, "girls don't know much; you poured it against his breath; of course he blew it up again."

"I poured it down his *throat;* how else could he swallow it?" said Tommy-Anne, resentfully, trying at the same time to wipe her hands on the grass.

"In his cheek pocket, outside his teeth, to be sure; when he opens to blow, it goes down. Give me what's left,—see; so." And with a rapid turn he emptied the bottle, and its contents disappeared within the astonished and disgusted

Waddles, who was then led to a soft hay bed, and left with only a large pan of water for company.

Tommy-Anne, feeling rather lonely without her usual companion, followed the Butcher's boy to the end of the garden, where he was setting out lettuce plants, and seating herself in the wheelbarrow nearby, prepared to have a nice long talk and hear about all the nests that he had found since she last saw him. She watched the boy crawl along; first making a small hole, by stabbing the earth with a pointed stick; then slipping a tiny seedling in the hole and squeezing the soil around it.

She opened her lips to call out, "Say, Butcher-boy!" when it occurred to her that, as he was to learn lessons with her father, and become a Naturalist, he might not like to be called Butcher-boy any longer, so she changed the question to, "What do they call you at home?"

"Bnb," he answered, neither stopping or looking up.

"Bub Bibbins; what a funny name!"

"'Tain't Bibbins."

"Isn't the Butcher your father?"

"Nope."

"Is he your uncle?"

" Nope."

" Who is he then, and why do you live with him ? "

" He's aunt's husband, and 'cause I can't help it."

" Whatever is the matter with him," thought Tommy-Anne; "he is as grumpy as cook was, when she broke her glasses and couldn't see, and tried to make the bread rise with a cracker instead of a yeastcake. I'll try again. Please is Bub your whole name, or only a pet name?"

" 'Tisn't a whole name, or a pet name; it is just a sort of kick-about, 'cause its handy. My real name is worse yet, — O-b-a-d-i-a-h, Obadiah Miles."

" Obadiah is rather choky to say, but," continued Tommy-Anne, brightening, " Obi is a nice fairy-story name. If I call you Obi, will you stop and talk to me ? "

The boy dropped his stick and sat up, wiping the drops of sweat from his face with the back of his hand — an act that left streaks of mud behind.

" Tommy-Anne," he said, " I'm not talking nowadays ; I'm working. Half-holidays I'll talk and make things, and show you the Duck's nest, if it isn't empty before I make time."

" Make time, how ? "

" I've got to *make* my half-holidays now, and
if you want me to have any, you must help and
not talk up the time. Your father said, ' Obadiah,' slow and reasonable, the way he always
talks, ' you'll have so much work to do every
week, and if you are quick about it, the time you
save is your own.' So you had better go away and
let me hustle, for those Wood Ducks won't be in
the shell a minute after Saturday, and I think
they are due to hatch Friday." As he saw her
disappointment he added, " I guess there is a Rabbit's nest, by now, over in the brush lot this side
of the woods, and now that Waddles is sick, you
might try to find it ; 'twouldn't do to take him
there."

To show that she understood, and to prevent
other words from escaping, Tommy-Anne shut
her lips together like a vise, and walked off
through the rough grass in which the garden path
ended. She did not half care to hunt for the
Rabbit's nest alone ; why not gather a bouquet of
tulips and ask Ruby-throat to take her to the
Flower Market? So she turned back and went
through the garden to the bed where the tulips
grew.

All the other spring bulbs were past and gone,
the hyacinths, daffies, and Duc Van Thols, but the

tall late tulips stood planted in a long row in front of the stone fence. Why, what was the matter with them? The flower stalks were drooping, and many plants lay withered on the earth, She knelt and lifted one ; it came up entirely, bulb and all, or rather it had no bulb, but merely the shell of one, the core having been eaten away from the bottom.

"It is those horrid moles!" she exclaimed. "They have eaten all mother's best double Dutch tulips, that father had sent from Holland for her birthday, and she was going to put them in the big blue jar and paint a picture of them, and now there are not enough left even for a bunch for Ruby-throat. It's too bad! I can see the hills that the nasty moles have kicked up all over." And Tommy-Anne pounded the ground with her fist.

" We did not eat the tulips," said a very squeaky voice coming from the earth in front of her. " We *never* eat vegetables, and we do not *kick* up our hills, or do anything so vulgar ; we *push* the earth out of our way with our hands."

" Who are you ? " said Tommy-Anne, putting her ear to the ground.

"One of the common Shrew Moles who live under your garden, and you have been saying whoppergrasses about us."

" What is a *whoppergrass?* "

" Whoppergrass is a word we have for a lie. It is that rank kind of grass that grows in bunches that the cows leave untouched ; it sticks in the throat, and not even a starving Rabbit can swallow it ; so when any one of us underground folk says something that his neighbours cannot swallow, we call it a whoppergrass."

" It *looks* as if you had eaten the bulbs, anyway, for there you are now close by them."

" Do you House People accuse each other of doing things for a little reason like that ? "

" Yes, very often, and Aunt Prue *always* does. It's what is called c-i-r-c-u-m-s-t-a-n-t-i-a-l evidence," father says, " judging from the way things look, you know."

" It's a very poor way ; in Heart of Nature's garden, things are mostly the way they don't look. In the first place, I told you that we don't eat vegetable food, and that should have settled the matter."

" What do you eat, then ? "

" Earthworms chiefly, yards and miles of them, and a great many other kinds of worms besides, — cut worms, grubs, slugs, and beetles. In fact, all sorts of underground things that otherwise would kill your plants and trees."

All of a sudden there was a loud squealing, and the earth was thrown up in a great furrow which caved in, showing two moles struggling with each other, then they rolled out on the walk. One dived quickly into his tunnel again, but the other being confused and bleeding at the nose, hesitated a minute. There was a large flower-pot standing near, and Tommy-Anne clapped it over him, saying, " Now you may stay under there, until you tell me all about yourself, and who *did* eat the tulips if you didn't."

The Mole, being very strong as well as obstinate, began to push the pot about with his paws, and even when Tommy-Anne sat on it to keep it still, she could feel it shake.

" Let me out," he cried, " and I will tell you ; but if you keep me here, I will dig down through the walk even if it is all gravel. Put me in the shade, please, and give me an earthworm. I feel rather faint, for that Star-nose bumped my nose terribly. He was a bully, for in underground etiquette it is not allowable to punch noses in fighting ; underground noses are made very sensitive for smelling the way."

He curled down in the shadow of the wall while Tommy-Anne found the worm, then he seized it, putting one end in his mouth and munched away, ramming it in with his paws as if he was feeding wood to a sawmill. Crunch, grit, crunch, went his jaws.

" What makes that queer noise? has an earthworm bones ? "

" The sand in the worm," said the mole. " Lots of the ground goes through the stomachs of earthworms. They break it up for things to grow in. By the way, my family name is de Rooter. I thought you might like to know it."

" What made you and the other Mr. de Rooter fly up out of the ground ? "

" We were fighting. The other mole was not of our colony, but a Star-nose, from the meadow. Somehow he came into our main tunnel and would not turn out for *me*, who made it. So we each tried to root the other out, and I forgot that we were in the top gallery and that the Star-noses are weak in the paws, and I pushed so hard that we both flew out together."

" Who is Star-nose ? "

" He is a cousin of ours, who lives deeper down

in the ground; his nose ends in a star-shaped flat, instead of a point, and he is a great fellow for smelling out things. His nest is deep, and he travels so low that he does not heave the turf ground as much as we do."

" If you don't eat them, I know that you *hurt* plants; for last summer you upset the bed of red geraniums and a long row of asters."

" Of course I may have done it when I was chasing worms, but it was an accident. Our hall-ways and passages do run under and between in the roots of things."

" How do you dig ? "

" We push the earth before us with our paws, as I said at first; and as it must go somewhere, if we are near the surface, it rises and makes the ridges that you see. Here is where the mischief happens to your bulbs; following us often in our tunnels, come the field mice, frisking and gambol-ling and gnawing and eating everything they can find, then whisking away again, leaving us to bear the blame.

" When Kabibonokka comes, Heart of Nature tells the frost to put an ice lock on the ground to keep it safely all the winter, letting nothing either out or in. But when Shawondasee and Kabibonokka fight, or Heart of Man, for some reason of his own and not understanding, interferes, the ice bolts are slipped.

" Last Moon of Snow-Shoes, the House People heaped up dry leaves over the tulip-bed, before the frost could lock the ground, thinking to keep it warm. Because of this the earth was soft, and we did not burrow deeply as we should when ice warns us to keep well down. In early spring the mice, hungry, as all things are at that time, came from their grass nests, through the wall chinks, into our runs, and nibbled at the bulbs, which kept on growing till their cores were reached, and then drooped and withered. Now if House People had not piled the leaves on until the ice locks were made fast, this would not have been. The use of covering is to hide the earth things from false awakenings, not to keep off the frost's locks.

" Kill the field mice, Tommy-Anne, and do not accuse the family of de Rooter again." And with a lunge he dived into one of the loose earth ridges.

" Humph ! " said Tommy-Anne, despondently; "that's all very well to say ' Kill the mice,' but it is what the Butcher's — no I mean Obi — calls a large contract. A hundred traps would not be enough for even the garden, and what good would they do when all out doors is *full* of mice? "

" We are here," hissed two voices. " We will catch the mice."

Tommy-Anne started in spite of herself. " Oh, it's you, is it," she said, as Lac and Lactina appeared, moving slowly by the wall. " I thought you promised never to startle me ? "

" We did not mean to ; we spoke before we came near ; what else could we do ? We have no rattles in our tails to give warning, like the Bad One."

" No, I suppose you did the best you could, but somehow you snakes always seem very sudden things. So you two think that you can catch all the mice, do you ? "

" Not all, perhaps, but a great many, and when they know that we live in the wall, the uneaten ones will be likely to move away. Besides, there will be our children, forty or fifty likely enough, before the summer is over, and there are a great many garter snakes about here too. We have eaten several small ones already, because they were in our way, but the big ones can help us with the mice."

" Then you are cannibals too, the same as Ko-ko-ko-ho and the Hawks ? "

" Oh yes, we eat small frivolous snakes, just as Whip, the black snake, eats us when he can.

Beware of letting Whip into your garden ! It is true that he eats rats and mice, but where Whip is at home, the Robin and Thrush mourn for their young, and no nest is sacred. We *prefer* mice and toads. See; we have each eaten a mouse this morning." And they stretched themselves so that she could see a lump that was between their throats and the middle of their bodies.

" I've seen a garter snake swallow a toad alive," said Tommy-Anne, "and I squeezed the snake with my spade, and made him unswallow, and the toad hopped off, after I poured a good deal of water on him. He was a little scrap bitten, but that was all."

"Yes, garter snakes do that, but you see how stupid they are ; for if they killed the toads first, then they could not get away."

Tommy-Anne sat thinking, and did not answer. One thing was certain : everything lived by eating some other thing.

" Don't you eat some other thing too ? " said Lactina, forking her tongue out to catch a fly that buzzed too near.

" I didn't speak," said Tommy-Anne, in astonishment.

" No, but I heard you think. We are a wise family, you know ; being constantly hunted has sharpened our wits."

"That's all very well, but I want you to remember one thing : I won't have too many of you about ; your children must move to other gardens, or I shall tell Obi about you. Two of you beside the garter snakes are quite enough."

Lac and Lactina disappeared under the wall, and Tommy-Anne still sat on the overturned flower-pot, thinking, and poking holes in the dirt with the toe of her shoe.

"Be careful, pray, be careful ; you are spoiling our village," said a voice, which was so faint that for a few minutes she could not tell from where it came.

"No ; we are not up in the air, nor among the flowers. Look down by your feet at the edge of the grass border. There you go again, making earthquakes ; you have shaken the nursery roof and made a hole in the cowshed wall already. *Do* take care ; it takes so long to build, and we are very busy now with all our spring work."

"Who are you, and *what* are you talking about?" said she, almost shouting, as if she thought the speaker must be deaf because its own voice was feeble.

"We are the field ants, whose village is under your grass border ; you, who wear the Magic Spectacles, can see us if you stoop down far enough."

Tommy-Anne lay flat on the border, so that the short grass looked to her like tiny trees; and she saw that amid this little forest was a sort of low earth hut, or hill, with a single doorway, and a great many paths leading to it. Bustling in and out, carrying little bundles and grains of sand, were countless small yellow ants.

"Put your eye to the door and look down; the houses are below," said an Ant who was somewhat larger than the rest.

Tommy-Anne did so, and found, to her surprise, that she could see, although it was dark. There were galleries leading to rooms whose roofs were held up by arches and pillars like those of a church, and the passage-ways were arched in the same manner.

In some of these rooms were little piles of what looked like kernels of grain, and in others, small green lice (such as we see on rose bushes) stood in rows, like horses in a stable.

"You see that we have carpenters and masons among us the same as they have in Birdland," said the big Ant.

"Did Ants make this beautiful cave?" asked Tommy-Anne, in amazement, afraid lest her breath should blow the sand about and break something.

M

"Our work-people built it all; they are those little ants that are now taking the eggs out to air."

"I see that there are different kinds and sizes of ants in your village; but don't you all work?"

"We big ants are the mothers; we lay the eggs and tend them also, when we are in a lonely village where help is scarce. The next in size are our husbands; they are usually rather delicate and sickly, and are short-lived, so they do not count for much; the smallest are the unmarried ants, and upon them falls the greater part of the work.

"Some of these are the masons and carpenters that build the villages. After carrying out the sand, grain by grain, to make room for the galleries, they bend the grass-blades and little roots for arches and supports, and mix sand with rainwater and dew to make the covering of mortar."

"What did you mean by saying that I was spoiling the nursery and cowshed?"

"This: we do not build nests like birds, and sit on our eggs until the warmth of our bodies hatches them. Our eggs are laid, a few in each of the little rooms we call the nurseries, and the nurse-ants have to carry them out every day so that the warmth of the sun may hatch them into grubs."

"What a piece of work!" sighed Tommy-Anne.

"Yes, it is a great deal of trouble, because if it grows too hot or rains they must all be brought in one by one and the holes covered carefully. Then as soon as the grubs are hatched they have to be fed until they spin into cocoons."

"Cocoons? Don't they hatch into ants right away?"

"Dear me, no. They come out of the egg as soft, legless grubs. These we feed with sweet liquids that we gather from the honeyed stalks of plants and milk from our cows."

"Cows? What sort of cows do ants keep?"

"The fat green plant-lice called aphides. We take them home and put them in the cowsheds that we build, and feed them well, and there they are all close at hand when we need their milk for our grubs."

"Is this *really truly?*" said Tommy-Anne, earnestly.

"It is perfectly true. Don't you see the rows of green cows down there, where you made a break in the wall?"

"Yes, — I do," said she, slowly, "but what happens when the grubs are fed and grow into cocoons?"

" They have to be carried in and out the same as when they were eggs, but when they are developed, the nurses break the threads of the cocoons, and the young ants appear. As soon as they are free, little gauzy wings begin to grow, but these drop off very soon after they are fully grown, and they become like the rest of us."

" Why do they need the wings if they fall off so soon ? "

" So that they can fly about and see the world and make new homes for themselves if they wish ; there is not room for all of them in the village where they are born."

" I should think that there would soon be too many ants."

" There might be, but for Birdland ; it eats so many of us and of our eggs, that there is no fear of that.

" Excuse me now, for I must see that our roof is mended before night."

Tommy-Anne stepped carefully away from the anthill and walked off toward the brush lot where the Rabbits lived. As she crossed a corner of the garden where a row of beans, as they sprouted, lifted the earth over their heads like a roof, she saw the tail of a small garter snake

that had been killed some days before, disappear
in the loose soil, while a large black and yellow
beetle was running round it, with lowered head,
scraping the earth with his feet, and pushing
with his claws.

"That is very queer," said Tommy-Anne, aloud,
halting as she spoke. "The snake was quite
dead two days ago ; it can't be moving of itself."

"Quite true ; it is dead, and we are burying
it," said the Beetle, who by this time was joined
by his mate, and both together they shovelled at
the earth until the tail entirely disappeared.

"Why do you take the trouble to do that?"
said Tommy-Anne."

"Because it is our trade. We are Sexton
Beetles," they answered proudly. "When any
small animal, like a snake or a mouse or a mole,
dies, we who live with our noses always close to
the ground know of it. Then we dig away
the earth beneath the thing, and push and
pull it down, until it is buried decently out
of sight."

"I think it is very good of you to work so hard
to keep the ground neat."

"Oh, we do not do it for neatness, though that
may be Heart of Nature's reason. He says, 'Bury,
that you may have food ready for your young

when they hatch, and lay your eggs beside what you bury.'"

"Food and eating!" exclaimed Tommy-Anne; "everything in Heart of Nature's garden seems to be for that."

"I have heard it said that even House People

eat several times a day," said the Sexton as he disappeared after the snake, leaving the ground perfectly smooth.

"I wonder if I shall ever get to the Rabbits," said Tommy-Anne, continuing on her way. "The air is always full of interesting people, and the trees, and the earth ; and to-day everything seems to be coming up from underground.

" Ah ! there is a Rabbit." And a pair of long, tawny ears lowered, and a fluffy cotton tail bobbed after them under a bush. Tommy-Anne chose a nice bit of turf under the shade of an old cedar, and sat down to watch. There were a great many cedar trees in the upper part of the lot, then a stretch of stubble and thick brush, before the alders and low willows marked the river.

In a few minutes a pair of ears peeped out of cover, then another pair, and another ; furry noses sniffed the air, and round eyes looked anxiously about. A whiff of wind shook the tall grasses : all the ears disappeared at once, but in a minute they had returned again.

" What makes you so scared ? " cried Tommy-Anne. " I'm not even thinking of hurting you, and I want you to be very nice and quiet, and tell me where you live, and lots of other things."

The bunnies scurried off again and held a consultation, and then the boldest returned and asked in a timid voice, " Where is the House Fourfoot ? "

" Waddles ? He is sick at home, very sick ; he won't be out for several days ; isn't it too bad ? "

If Tommy-Anne expected them to be sorry, she very soon discovered her mistake, for at the news, which spread like fire in dry grass, the whole field was full of rabbits. Young and old, hopping, dancing, and doing the grand chain up and down; while one big Jack, the strong man of the warren, turned a summersault and stood erect, using the tips of his ears for legs.

Tommy-Anne screamed with laughter, which sound had the effect of scattering the dancers; big Jack, however, remained, and a few others huddled around him.

"You seem to be glad that poor Waddles is ill," she said presently. "Does he often chase you? If he does, I shall speak to him about it."

"Chase us? Yes, indeed he does; but, worse than that, he lies in wait for us to pass by and jumps out and frightens us half to death, for fun, and not when he is hungry. Last season we could not cross the Miller's meadow, because Waddles was always hiding in the long grass."

"Oh, ho! that was why he made all those nests! Crafty Waddles! Tell me why you always jump about so at every little sound."

"Our ears are so long that even a little noise seems very loud to us, and we are always on the jump, because running to our holes is the only

way we have of escaping from our enemies, for
we can neither fly nor fight."

"Where do you live?"

"In long earth tunnels and under hollow
stumps. In winter, we try to make doorways
where the ice shall not lock us in, for we do
not store up food like the squirrels, nor yet
sleep the long winter sleep like Father Woodchuck."

"But what can you find to eat in winter even
if you are not frozen in?"

"Buds, twigs, and the sprouts of soft little
things that wait for Shawondasee, near the
surface. We keep the bushes and low sweeping
trees well pruned, but we seldom eat their roots."

"In summer you come in the garden and eat
the young lettuce and cabbage leaves, for father
says that he has *seen* you."

"Perhaps, — yes, — I think we did; but then,
when you planted much more lettuce than you
ever used, how did we know but that you meant
it for us?"

"Do your children live in the burrows?"
asked Tommy-Anne, fearing that she was
being cornered.

"Not at first; we make ground hollows for
their cradles when they are born. There is my

nursery, yonder, between those wild rose bushes. If you wish, you may come and look at it."

Tommy-Anne willingly followed him. When they reached the spot, she could see nothing at first but brown grass, for the young rabbits were so nearly the colour of the earth, leaves, and whisps of fur that made the nest. Presently she distinguished four pairs of bright eyes. The mother Wabasso came hopping up at that minute, and whispered joyfully to Jack.

"We can go to the garden. House Fourfoot is shut up." But she looked extremely foolish when she saw Tommy-Anne standing there, and settled down in the nest to suckle her babies.

"Will you give me two of those to keep in my rabbit house, when Obi builds it?" asked Tommy-Anne.

"You may have them and welcome, but they would burrow out and come back to us. The Gray Rabbit loves his liberty even better than ease and good eating. Cat rabbits are the best kind for your house."

"What are cat rabbits?"

"The black, white, and spotted ones who have fur like cats. You can see them if they run away; but we are furred like the wreckage of tree and bush that litters the ground."

After Tommy-Anne had left the rabbits and turned to cross the field, she could still hear them whispering.

"She is going to keep tame rabbits in her garden," said Wabasso; "what will Fourfoot say to that?"

"I wonder what the cabbages will look like," chuckled Jack. "One good thing: Fourfoot will have plenty of things to chase near home, and *we* can *eat* the lettuce, and *they* will bear the blame!"

"Waddles is not popular with ground beasts," said Tommy-Anne, emphatically. "What shall I do now? I think I will go to the river woods and see if I can find the Wood Duck's nest by myself."

"Bum-m-m, bumbelty-um-um-m! That would be very mean when Obi is working to make time to show it to you," said a big black, gold-trimmed, Bumble-bee, flying in her face and making her start and wink.

"I don't think it concerns you one single bit," she said rather crossly. First because the bee frightened her, and secondly because she knew, without being told, that it would not be kind to go without Obi, and did not like to be reminded of it.

"Certainly it concerns me. Am I not Gitche-ah-mo, the great Busy Bee? Everybody's business is mine."

"Where are you going?" asked Tommy-Anne, as much to change the subject as because she cared to know, when the bee blundered from a grass stalk to the ground and began to disappear.

"Home," said Mr. Bumble, stopping a minute.

"Do you live underground? I thought tame bees lived in hives, and wild ones in tree hollows."

"Honey bees do; but there are a great many other kinds beside them."

"Don't you make honey?"

"A little to eat during the warm season, but we do not store it away like the others. Those of us who live all winter sleep and do not need it."

"What do you find to do all day if you don't pack away honey?"

"We work in the Flower Market, carrying the precious dust from flower to flower, to help fill the seed lunch baskets. This is our mission — everywhere from the hot countries, to the northland where the flowers stop blooming at the snow's very edge."

"Do you have hives underground?"

"Not hives, but little chambers.   We are soli-
tary bees, and even our colonies hold scarcely
more than half a hundred of us, while the honey
bees swarm by thousands.   Yet in spite of this
you will always find some of us in every Flower
Market, and we never dart at you to sting.

"My eggs are hatching now, a foot or two
below the ground, and the workers are tending
them.   Good-bye for now; but you will find
me any day in the Flower Market."

"I was going there to-day, but the field mice
ate the tulips that the Oak said I must give Ruby-
throat for his breakfast, when I asked him to
take me there."

"Wait a few days and give him roses instead.
Remember that the Rose Family is the most
useful in the whole Flower Market, and the
most powerful as well."   And Mr. Bumble was
off before Tommy-Anne could even think another
question.

It was nearly noon, and she thought Waddles
must be lonely, and that she would go back to see
him.   Tommy-Anne was climbing lazily over the
stone fence back of the garden, when a very puffy
toad on the opposite side attracted her attention
by the violent gestures he was making.

"What do you want?" she said, half jokingly;

"it seems to me that all the underground people are out walking to-day."

"I have a petition to give you, from all the toads in the cellar and gar-den," said Mr. Puffy, swelling his leathery throat with im-portance.

"A petition? That is the thing that people write and ask some one else to carry, when they want some-thing of some-body and don't quite like to speak out and ask for it themselves. Very well, give it to me," said Tommy-Anne, in a tone quite as solemn as the toad's.

"It isn't written," he said, somewhat abashed; "for we can't write. I'm to speak it, you see."

"Speak it then, but be quick, for it is very hot here."

"I know it is, for toad blood is so cold, and I am accustomed to living so much in the damp and shade, that I feel quite giddy, but I *had* to see you.

"To shorten a long story, the fact is that we do not wish to have Lac and Lactina live in the garden under your protection, for it makes them so bold that we are very unhappy. They steal up behind us when we are out fly-catching, and poke into our holes when we are at home, breaking up our family parties.

" We are friends to the garden, as much as they are; we stay here from the time our young grow their legs, down in the watercourse, until Frost drives us underground, and we catch many hurtful bugs and worms. Is it fair that we should be driven away and eaten by snakes? We beg you either drive away the snakes or protect us also."

" Oh dearie me! What shall I do about this?" said Tommy-Anne; "here are two things that are both good for the garden, and yet one eats the other!"

" Do nothing. Leave all such things to me," said a voice seeming to come from nowhere, but sounding everywhere.

" That sounds like my dear Tree Man's voice, only there is no tree near for him to live in," said Tommy-Anne, half aloud.

" The Tree Man does not live in a tree to-day. Heart of Nature travels with his friend Shawondasee, the South Wind."

" I wanted to make everything happy," she explained.

"I know that, Tommy-Anne; but Heart of Man can only help me when he understands the reasons of the Plan, and when he does not understand, the best thing that he can do is to keep his own hands from killing, and to wait! Watch through the Magic Spectacles, but do not interfere with me; for you know nothing, not even how to build a sparrow's nest. There are other animals to keep the snakes from over-running the earth, as the snakes keep the toads down, and the birds control the bugs and worms, and so on upward."

"I have my eyes on the snakes, you know," said a Weasel, poking his sharp nose out of the wall.

Tommy-Anne returned to the place where she had left Obi planting lettuce. He had finished; the long rows were covered with slanted boards to keep the sun out, and he was scraping the clay off his shoes, whistling cheerfully all the time.

" Did you find the rabbits ? " he asked.

" Yes, and lots of other things ; I never knew that so many things lived underground."

" How about the roots of everything, and the springs of water ? "

" To be sure," said Tommy-Anne.

" I'm going to my lessons now, but I'll tell you a secret : I can work fast enough to earn *all* Saturday afternoon to look for the Duck's nest ! "

" Splendid ! " cried Tommy-Anne, her eyes shining. " And perhaps Waddles will be well by that time ; he is *so* interested in ducks."

" Waddles stays at home when I go to watch ducks hatch," said Obi, decidedly.

" Please tell me one thing before you go in the house," pleaded Tommy-Anne. " Is it true that moles only eat worms and bugs, and never eat plants ? "

" Yes, of course it is."

" How do you know ? "

" Opened lots of moles that have been caught in traps, to see what they ate," said Obi, settling the question.

" Let me out, mistress," whined Waddles, through the woodhouse door. " My cold was horrid enough by itself, and the physic was worse, but being shut up in here, where I can't

N

see or smell what is going on, will give me a high fever."

"So it always does me, Waddlekins; but then, staying in when you have taken physic is a *must be!*"

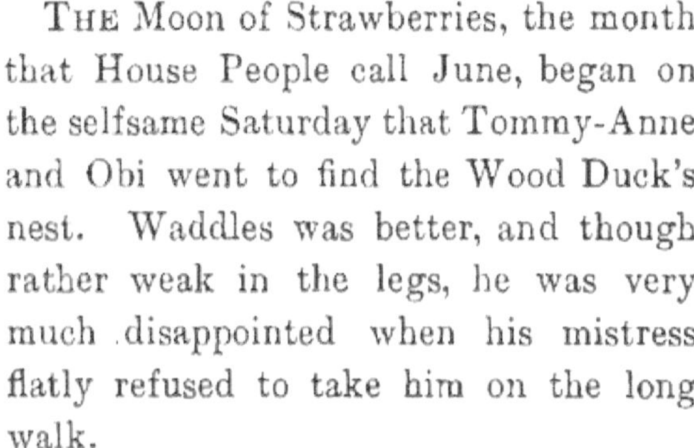

IX

ASPETUCK

THE Moon of Strawberries, the month
that House People call June, began on
the selfsame Saturday that Tommy-Anne
and Obi went to find the Wood Duck's
nest. Waddles was better, and though
rather weak in the legs, he was very
much disappointed when his mistress
flatly refused to take him on the long
walk.

"We are going a great way up the
river; there will be rocks and bushes
in the way; and you would be sure to
get your feet sopping wet, Waddlekins
dear," said Tommy-Anne; "so you see
that you are better off at home."

"*I* see very plainly, mistress, that you are going hunting, and it is for something that you don't wish me to see." And Waddles put on his saddest expression. But it was of no use; the door of the woodhouse closed, and his feelings were doubly injured by hearing the key turned. Then Tommy-Anne's feet went patter, patter down the road as she ran to join Obi, who had been waiting for her by the turnpike bridge for some time.

"Do not run so fast, little daughter," called her father, from the study window; "you have plenty of time. Obi has earned a whole holiday, and your mother has given him a basket of luncheon for you both."

Tommy-Anne instantly rushed to the window, and threw handfuls of kisses, calling, "You dear, *dear* father-mother!"

She had often used this term, when she spoke of her father and mother at the same time, ever since one day, when she was a very small child, some foolish person had asked her which she loved best, her father or her mother; when she answered indignantly, "Which? they aren't a *which;* father-mother is the same person!"

"See the tadpoles," said Obi, who was kneeling by the pool above the bridge, and watching some

little dusky shapes that darted through the water.
"Their legs have sprouted, but their tails haven't
gone yet."

"What are tadpoles?" asked Tommy-Anne,
also kneeling, and looking at the queer things
with oblong bodies, and narrow finny tails, while
two arms seemed to be budding out in front, and
two legs behind.

"Tads are young frogs; it is the way they look
a little while after they are hatched. The frogs'
eggs are hung on the leaves of water-plants,
and when the eggs are first hatched they seem
like leaves themselves; then they begin to float
about in the water, growing all the time and
changing. Tails sprout, and then legs; and as
the legs grow bigger, the tail grows smaller,
until it all turns into legs, and the tad is a frog,
ready to hop."

"Oh yes! and then they hop over to the swamp,
and cry, 'Bree-r! Bree-r!' all night long."

"Not this kind; those are tree-frogs, but these
are children of the big bull-frogs that live in
ponds."

"Dahinda's children. He is ugly and fat, but
these children are positively silly," said Tommy-
Anne, as one came to the surface and took a long
breath, which she mistook for a yawn. "Do

tadpoles ever swallow themselves?" she asked, wondering at the size of its mouth.

"Now, Tommy-Anne, suppose you think a minute; how could they! If they swallowed themselves, where would they be swallowed into?"

Of course she could not tell, and Obi continued to laugh at her as they wandered up the river, peering in the rocky crevices and poking into holes with their sticks.

"See that bit of wood, underneath this stump in the deep pool," said Tommy-Anne. "It keeps close to the bottom; why doesn't it float?"

Obi looked a minute, and then lay down flat on his stomach, motioning for her to keep very still. "It isn't a stick, it's a big pickerel," he whispered; "but it wants the little perch to think that it is a stick, and come near enough to be eaten. Watch out now!"

Two of these careless fish were swimming lazily down stream, gaping and gazing idly from side to side. A flash and a snap! The surface of the water eddied, and one of the little fishes was in the mysterious inside of Mr. Pickerel, who steadied himself by two or three motions of his tail, and pointed his nose to the bank, silently as before.

"What a biter that pickerel is!" exclaimed Tommy-Anne.

"Biter? I should say he was. Look a-here!" Obi showed some round white scars that made a line across the ends of his left hand fingers. "One of those fellows did that to me, way back in the spring. I hooked him for keeps, and he thought the smartest thing he could do would be to swallow me, so he began with those fingers."

"It is lovely, here by the water," said Tommy-Anne, after a few minutes, drawing a long breath of contentment; "everything is so new and green; and there are simply acres of ferns in there. Do look yonder; they climb up hill as far as we can see!"

"Yes, the ferns are bully!" said Obi, approvingly; "but *we* are after the Duck's nest, and when you come to the woods, if you don't find what you started after *first*, the other things will make you forget all about it. I'll tell you what we can do. Suppose I take the lunch basket and find the easiest way to the Duck's tree and come back for you. I generally go round the other way by the foot of the mountain, but that is a rough place, and I am not pop sure where we strike it from this side."

"That will be very nice," said Tommy-Anne, "for there are plenty of things for me to look at here." She was very glad to be left alone, for there were several questions that she wished to ask the river, but did not care to have Obi see that she could, or have him know about the Magic Spectacles, for they were a secret between Heart of Nature and herself.

"Who are you?" she asked, trailing her fingers lightly through the water, which answered her touch like a live thing.

"I am your Water Brother; without me you could not live," it answered softly, humming a little tune as it tumbled over the pebbles, then growing silent as it neared the Pickerel's pool.

"Next to Light, which is the twin brother of Heat, I am the oldest thing in the world. Heart of God fashioned us three from his own being and then making the Plan, gave it to Heart of Nature to work out, saying: —

"'Here are the beginnings that I have created; follow now my plan through the long timeless days that I give you for its development. Go upward, little by little; from shapelessness to form, from the grass to the tree, from the creeping reptile to the great beasts; but pause thou there, for to complete my share I will create

anew and stamp the animal who is to be the
ruler of this globe of mine with my own coin-
age.   He shall be called Heart of Man, and,
though the youngest thing of all, he shall be the
bond betwixt thee and me, for two natures shall
be in him, — mine and thine.

"' Born shall he be according to thy laws,
O Heart of Nature, my servant, and die, seem-
ingly, after thy way; but he wears my image
as a spark within him, and when he dies, only
your part returns to you, — my part, my coin-
age, returns to me, its Home.   And thus my
seal-mark separates him from all other animals,
for this seal-mark is the Soul!'

"Then we three forces began to work, with
Heart of Nature as interpreter of the Plan, and
finally, when Heart of Man came, time came
with him, and he set his measurements and
said, 'I will divide off spaces for convenience'
sake; so much time shall be a day, a month, a
year.'   But before man all was the Eternity of
Heart of God.   Simple as all this is, House
People *will* make things hard to understand, because they ignore the Plan, and measure everything from their own end and test by their own
plan, instead of Heart of God's.

"Still through it all I am your Water Brother;
I am here, there, everywhere, — in the rain clouds,
in the rainbow that follows them; I am the sea
itself, holding the earth in my embrace; I am
in the tree blood and in your own blood, flowing,
always flowing, and I am the emblem of the life
that shall be."

There was not a sound for a moment; the river
and Tommy-Anne each waited for the other to
speak, then the river broke the stillness.

"I cannot keep quiet long when I come in this
shape," he laughed; "for here, I am only a bab-
bling bit of a Water Brother, and though I never
forget my origin and history, my work now is with
small things. Here, I am a very tattler and a
tell-tale. I am a bearer of trivial news, carrying
messages from my birthplace, all the way down
to the last water gate, where the salt enters my
veins.

"So I wander along, giving drink to the Fox
and Coon, a bath to the Hawk and Hummingbird
alike; turning the wheel for the Miller, making
pools for the big fish and sweeping the little ones
into my shallows where their enemies may not
follow. Everything brings me news, which I repeat to the Wind if there is no one else near to

listen. Tell-tale, tell-tale, the pebbles make me call; the pebbles that are the rock fragments I have polished for my bed.

" Listen ! as I pass the stony places you can hear me singing tell-tale, tell-tale, for days together; but though I am a gossip, I am wise enough never to tell *all* that I know, for some things belong to Silence ! "

" Yes," answered Tommy-Anne ; " I can understand what you are singing now, but all the spring you have been roaring and scolding so, that I could not make out a single word."

" I am not answerable for what I do in the spring," said the river, shrugging his shoulders until they were covered with foam ; " in the spring I am really not quite myself. A lot of strange snow water comes racing down the hills into my course, and I grow quite mixed up and I know that I misbehave ; I always do. Only last month, there was such a crowd of water tramps, all from different places, trying to go to the sea by my roadway, that we lifted the old turnpike bridge on our shoulders and set it down again, above the pond in the Miller's meadow.

" Then, when we heard that the road-menders were coming to try and take it back again, we rushed down that night and gave the old thing a shaking that scattered its ribs along the banks and sent its backbone into the sluice-way, nearly choking the mill to death.   It was such fun !"

" What made you do that?   I should call it mischief, not fun."

" No, it was fun, and like fun usually, it had wisdom at the bottom of it.   The turnpike needed a new bridge, for I could see the sun through the great holes in it.   Last summer Gheezis said to me, 'I will do all I can to dry this bridge ; do you tell the rains to hurry and rust the nails so that they will fall out, and then you can wash it away, for it is no longer safe.' "

" That is true," said Tommy-Anne ; " our horse put his foot through one of the holes and father spoke to the Selectmen about it, but they only put on a worn old board for a patch.   I think you are a very clever little river.   Please have you any name?"

" Aspetuck is my name here; the Red Brothers gave it to me, and it means that I come from a height.   In fact, for the first three miles of my life I do nothing but run down hill, stopping every now and then in some little corner to get my breath."

" How did you begin?   Were you a brook or a pond, or did you rain down suddenly and run along ? "

"My beginnings were smaller than either of these. I was only a moist spot, on the top of a hill, a bit of grass touched by the Water Spirit. Around me were other moist places which, like myself, could not move, and when the sun shone on us, we grew less and less. I heard the trees rustle and the notes of the birds, but I did not understand them, and they could not see me. The grass that grew about me was a little greener because of my presence, and the small ferns sucked my moisture greedily, but that was all.

"One day the earth, by heating and cooling, added a few more drops to me, then rain fell and gave me new vigour, when the sun burst out again I leaped to meet it, and, without knowing how, I escaped down the hillside.

"Life, motion, how delicious they were! Presently a Song-Sparrow who had been singing in the open field came and bathed in me, spattering my drops far and wide. It was an anxious moment; for, thought I, if he uses up too much of me, there will not be enough to go onward.

"This danger passed, I ran along until I reached some trees, and I wondered how I could ever climb over their high roots. 'Avoid them,' said Heart of Nature; 'go between, and remem-

ber, little brook, your happiness will depend
greatly upon knowing *what* to avoid.'

"Then the Birth Spirits thronged about me,
offering their gifts. The meadows promised me
free passage through the fields and lowlands, with
beds of moss, bordered with Iris, and a gay escort
of flowers all through the season. For lancers,
it would give the stately spiked

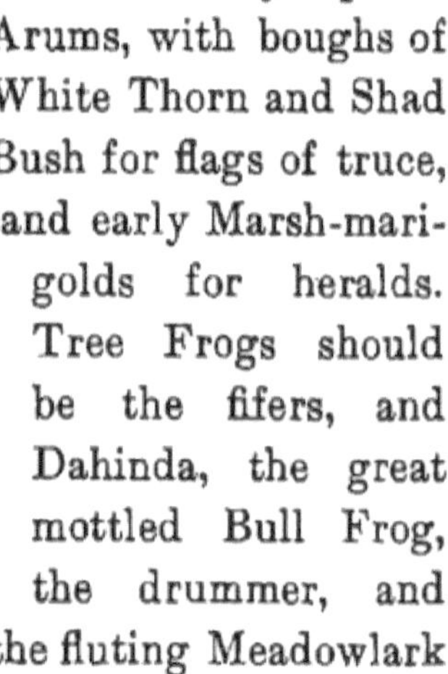

Arums, with boughs of
White Thorn and Shad
Bush for flags of truce,
and early Marsh-mari-
golds for heralds.
Tree Frogs should
be the fifers, and
Dahinda, the great
mottled Bull Frog,
the drummer, and
the fluting Meadowlark
and madcap Bobolink the minstrels.

"Heart of Nature said, 'These are beautiful
things, and they have their places ; but remember
also to bear with you, as you flow, all the un-
cleanness that would make my garden foul, for
to wash away and purify is one of the duties
of water.'

"The Spirit of the Woods was the Birth Spirit

that I loved the best. It wore the shape of sweeping Hemlocks, who guided me between the jutting rocks and swayed as they bent above, crooning my cradle song. Many stories they told me, and legends that they only speak between themselves, when they twist and threaten, defying all the winds, even Kabibonokka himself. When I slipped from their arms, they moaned and cried, 'Do not forget us when you are a river! Do not forget those who rocked your cradle!' I promised, but when I saw them next, alas! I was filled with sorrow.

"But then I was full of pride. Humph, I thought, *when you are a river*! What am I now, pray, but a river? And I fretted at the tall grasses that would not move for me, until I was all afoam and thought that an oak leaf that fell on me was one of the ships that the Hemlocks talked about. In hurrying around the corner of a rock, I met half a dozen other streams like myself, who said they were travelling together until they should become a river; and as I could not turn back, I joined them, but feeling quite discouraged to find how small I really was.

"Heart of Nature whispered, 'Do not be discouraged; no one thing in the Plan is anything of itself but depends always upon some other thing.'

And I knew that he was right. What was one drop of water? Yet the river and the ocean are only a great many such drops.

"'Brotherhood,' said Heart of Nature, 'that is the password.'

"After that I understood everything that I heard and saw. At the shallow places the birds bathed and chattered, and I heard a Flycatcher complain that the snakes shed their skins in such thorny places that he could not pull them out for nest-building."

"Why do snakes shed their skins? and are they not very naked without them?"

"They shed them when they are shabby and old, just as the birds moult their feathers, only *under* the old skin is a bright new one, and all they have to do is to crawl out of the old one through the mouth hole, and there they are in a fresh dress, leaving the old rag in the bushes behind them.

"When I came along between shady banks, I heard a great many complaints from growing things, who wished me to ask justice for them. The Ferns complained because they had no pretty, easy names, such as flowers bear, to keep them in the remembrance of House People."

"Ferns are only ferns," said Tommy-Anne.

" Why do they need names? Some are large, and some small ; but they are very much alike, except the Maidenhair, and that has a name already."

" There it is again ; you are like all the rest," sighed a tall, handsome Brake, bending over Tommy-Anne's shoulder. " We are as unlike each other as any two flowers in your garden ; and though we have no showy blossoms, we hold the little seed lunch baskets on the backs of our leaves, or on stalks by themselves. We carpet the forest, and, with our cousins, the mosses, cover the rocks ; but even the Red Brothers neglected to name us, and we have lost hope."

" I will tell Obi about you,— that may do some good," said Tommy-Anne ; " for he is going to be a wise man and learn everything about wild things, and perhaps some day he will think of some easy names for you. I wonder if he has found the Duck's nest yet," said Tommy-Anne, turning to Aspetuck.

" Yes, he has found it ; but it is two miles above here, and it is on the other side of the river. He has crossed the stepping-stones, and is half-way back already."

" Do you know about everything that happens along your banks?"

"Everything. At this moment, above the third bridge, some cows are wading across; at the mill farm they are washing cans; they should not wash milk cans in me — I carry off too much wastage to be fit for that. By the second bridge, in the deep hole, some little boys are swimming. They will soon have bad cramps, for the chill of the snow has not yet wholly left me. A pair of water-snakes have fallen from a grape-vine quite near where you are sitting, and swim down stream. No! do not start, for they are harmless, even if they are quarrelsome and wear ugly grizzled coats.

"Hark! one thing more is happening!" said Aspetuck. "They are sawing wood at the upper mill. How well I remember the day that I learned for the first time what this mill was, and found that I must turn the wheel that rent my old friends, the Hemlocks, into boards. There they lay, barkless, on the bank. This was my first grief! Good-bye, Tommy-Anne; I must hurry down to the grist mill, to grind some corn that is wanted for your cows, and after that I have to sow seed along my banks.

"Do I sow seed? Yes, that I do; the winds, the birds, and I sow more than any other husbandmen in Nature's garden. We may not plant our crops in even drills and great fields, like House People, but we are the makers of both the Northern Forest and the Southern Jungle. You have geranium beds on your lawn, and I the beds of lilies in my ponds, — that is all the difference."

"How is it, dear Aspetuck, that you go away and yet you are still here?"

"Ah! you must ask that question of Wabeno, the Magician. I am a mystery, —all the time passing by, yet the whole of me is never any-where, because part of me is everywhere," said the river, laughing merrily at her wonderment.

Tommy-Anne listened for the sound of Obi's footsteps, and, as she could not hear them, she walked back a little way from the river, and seated herself upon a stump. As she did so, a tall, coarse weed beside her cried, "Don't touch me! I sting! I am a Nettle!"

"Ugh!" said Tommy-Anne, drawing back. "I am much obliged to you for telling me; the only nettles I know about are very much smaller than you."

"I am the Wood-Nettle, and my cousin the great Fence-Nettle is twice as big as I am, almost as tall as a House Man. His prickles are not as sharp as mine, but he will make you smart if you are heedless enough to fall from some tumbledown fence into his clutches. But if you ever do, remember to put some fresh earth on the spot, and it will take the pain away."

Dry twigs crackled, and in another minute Obi appeared, in a state of elation, for he had found the Duck's nest, and the Ducks were hatched, and would soon leave to go down to water. He was carrying a thick snake that he had killed, holding it carefully by the tip of its tail.

"*Please* drop that horrid thing, Obi," screamed Tommy-Anne. "I'm sure it is one of those wicked rattlesnakes."

"Oh no, it isn't. I killed it on purpose to show you the difference, so that you need not be afraid of them; for there are plenty of this kind hereabouts. Don't shiver and shake so; it's stone dead, even if it was a rattler. Come and look at him."

Tommy-Anne, thus persuaded, drew nearer. The first thing that she noticed was that the snake's nose was blunt and horny; then she saw that the head was flat and thick, while its wide, mottled brown body ended in a stumpy tail.

"What sort of a snake is it?" she asked.

"A Hog-nose. Round here we mostly call them blowing adders, 'cause when they are mad they blow up their necks and hiss. They are lazy things, they can't go very fast, and often play dead to make people go away and let them alone, rather than take the trouble to move."

"Obi, are you perfectly *sure* it is a Hog-nose?" asked Tommy-Anne, anxiously. She had pried open its mouth with a stick, and found that it had some large teeth that looked like fangs.

"You see that it has no pit-mark below its eyes, as our poison snakes have. I'm going to keep this snake and make a skelly of it, so that you can see how its bones work, and its fangs and all that."

"Then you had better hang it up in a tree, or the Sexton Beetles may come and bury it for you."

"That is so," said Obi; "I guess I'll take it with me, for some Owl might come by and grab it out of the tree." And they hurried off, Obi telling about the Ducks, who had chosen a new nesting-place across the river, as a Cat Owl had appropriated the old tree.

Such a pretty place as the Wood Ducks had chosen for their home, — close by a pond, where the river had been widened to feed a mill. The old building, with its great wooden water-wheel, was standing yet, on a mossy, stone foundation. Everything about was mossy; every crack held a fern, and all the banks were covered with laurels and blooming wild azaleas.

"See, I left the lunch basket here on this flat rock; it will make a jolly table," said Obi. "We mustn't talk any more now, but only whisper. The Duck's tree is round on the other side, and if we go into the mill, we can look almost into the nest from the window. Here, creep along this beam, — so — the floor is very rotten, but I've fixed a place by the window where we can stand."

Yes, there were some bits of board, secured so that the children could stand comfortably and look through the twisted sash, and yet be perfectly hidden. The nest tree was a chestnut that had lost many branches, and in the stump of one of them, nearly twenty feet from the ground, there was a hollow, from which was sticking some ends of grass and feathers.

"The nest is in there," said Obi, rather by signs than words.

"No," signalled Tommy-Anne, "the place is too small for a duck to live."

"She lives there, all the same," nodded Obi.

"How will she ever get the ducklings down? They will break their necks."

This time Obi only answered by putting his finger to his lips, for then something happened. A beautiful plump Duck (with a gray head and neck, a small shining green crest, brown back, and mottled gray breast) flew along, giving a cry that sounded like peek-peek oc-eek! and disappeared in the hollow branch.

"Is that the father duck?"

"No," whispered Obi; "the father is twenty times handsomer,—all red and purple and green, with a long cockatoo on his head; but he is a selfish pig, and goes off as soon as the eggs are laid; he doesn't like babies."

While they were whispering, half of a smooth clay-coloured egg-shell rolled out of the hole, and the mother appeared holding a downy duckling in her beak. She climbed with her sharp claws to the top of the branch, spread her wings and dropped to the ground, left her burden at the foot of the tree, and returned to the hole.

Nine times she flew down, bringing a duckling, which she placed with its brothers and sisters. On the tenth trip, as she left the hole, a second nestling climbed on her back; but she reached the ground successfully with her double load, and once there, walked off to the pond, her brood following her through the bushes and into the water, as if they had done the same thing every day for a month. In a moment some little noise startled the family, and they dived and disappeared, probably going beyond the turn in the pond.

"Is not that won-d-e-r-ful!" said Tommy-Anne, lost in admiration.

"I'm going to look in the nest to see if there are any eggs that didn't hatch," said Obi, "and then we can have our dinner."

"Tale-to-tell, tale-to-tell!" called Aspetuck from below; "look at Waddles, on the rock!"

Tommy-Anne jumped up so quickly that she almost fell through a hole in the floor, and hurried out to where they had left the luncheon. There sat Waddles by the basket, tired, muddy, and very forlorn.

"How did you get out, you bad dog?" said his mistress, stamping her foot.

"Dug a hole under the door," whined the culprit; "the earth told me the way as far as the other side of the river, and then I saw the basket." And he sniffed and looked unspeakable things with his big brown eyes, now really heavy and sad. "It was *very* hard digging, mistress."

"Don't you know that you have been sick, and that it cost the whole of one of father's dollars to pay the Blacksmith for coming to see you, and you will never be able to earn a dollar?"

Waddles seemed crushed, and did not answer except by wagging his tail.

Then Tommy-Anne simply *had* to laugh, he looked so pitiful, and said, "Never mind for this time, because I can't whip a sick dog, even if he *is* bad. You shall have the top lid of my sandwiches for your dinner, and perhaps Obi will be kind enough to carry you home."

And Waddles was so meek, that he seemed pleased with bread and butter, which he usually scorned.

After dinner followed a great hunt for wild-flowers, turtles, and tree-toads, and then the question was how to get home. Obi had found three eggs in the Duck's nest that would never hatch; then there was the snake, the lunch basket, a snake skin, a small snapping turtle that Tommy-Anne had found, and Waddles, who was really used up by his trip, his front and back legs going in different directions when he tried to walk.

"Put the eggs in the basket with the snake skin, tie a string to the tail of the Hog-nose, and I will carry him too. Then you can put my turtle in your pocket and carry Waddles; he will be a big enough load for you."

"But I'm not as fat as I *was*," sighed Waddles, as the procession started, looking over Obi's shoulder and thinking it a great disgrace to be carried. They marched home in single file, and Tommy-Anne wondered why her parents laughed so heartily when she stopped under the study window to call, "We've come home, father-mother, and we've had a spl-e-n-did time ! "

But when she went up stairs to make herself neat for tea, she saw the reason. "Umph ! " she said, "I look just like a moulting chicken." Which was a fact; for the heel was off one shoe, half of her hat brim hung down in a loop, her hair was full of twigs, and her blouse was torn across the back.

"Never mind," she said, struggling with her

brush; "my hair will-just-have-to-let-itself-be-unsnarled, and to-day was worth my very best gown, and this was only a very *weakly* blouse, anyway." And as she toiled and struggled with her tangled mane, she could hear her Water Brother across the road singing to the pebbles.

X

THE FLOWER MARKET

IN these June days Tommy-Anne visited the rose-bed every morning the first thing after break-

fast, and she watched the buds so closely that Obi said if she was not careful she would look holes through them. One morning, however, a great straggling bush, with small dark green leaves, was completely covered with pale yellow flowers, that opened rather flatly, showing the golden fringe at the heart.

Tommy-Anne ran to the bush in delight, and buried her face in the nearest cluster, but drew back even more quickly, her dear little pug nose turning up with an injured expression as if it had been cruelly cheated, as she said, "*You* will never do for Ruby-throat's breakfast; you smell a-w-fully, and your thorns sting like nettles. Wouf!" And she shuddered and wiped the afflicted member with a large red cotton handkerchief.

She preferred these handkerchiefs above any other sort. In the first place, they did not lose themselves easily, a matter of great importance; then she could carry almost anything in them that she could lift,—from eggs, fruit, and such like, to mossy stones and clumps of ferns. They also made admirable towels, when she had been fishing with her hands for tadpoles or frogs, or wading in the river, and lastly they made very effective signal flags.

Next morning brought better luck. Jacque-minot buds began to peep out from their cool dark green leaves, and one great pink cabbage rose had slipped its roundness from the five green claws that held it in bud. Here was quite enough for a bouquet.

Selfish Tommy-Anne! Her father, who was also watching the roses, came through the garden, cut the pink beauty and its long stem with one flash of his knife, and carried it indoors to her mother. Of course the red roses *would* do, but Ruby-throat might have felt more complimented by the larger flower ; or he might have a choice in roses, and prefer pink to crimson. ' Well, it could not be helped.

Obi was coming through the fields towards the garden ; he had something in his hand. "Was it ? Could it be ? " thought Tommy-Anne. Yes, he was carrying a bunch of early wild roses, and in a second they came flying over the fence toward her, and Obi turned into the cart track that led to the barnyard.

"Thank you, thank you e-v-e-r so much ! " called Tommy-Anne, waving her handkerchief as a joy signal. " Where d-i-d you get them ? "

Obi did not seem to hear the question. A great change had come over him since he had been allowed to study at Happy House (for this was the name Tommy-Anne had given her home). She noticed that he was very deaf in working hours, but recovered his hearing entirely on holidays.

" Now I have enough for a bouquet," she said, unfastening the wild roses, which were tied with more than a yard of stout string into a turnip-like lump, and doing them up prettily with a red bud stuck in here and there ; " I wonder why Obi made such a cabbagey bouquet."

" He made it to *throw* well," said a thin voice close to her ear. " If you tried to throw yours,

it would go as many ways as there are flowers
in it."

A whirring noise followed the voice ; a sound
such as the wheels of an alarm clock make before
it strikes.   Then there was a flutter, a gleam of
emerald and gold, and Tommy-Anne saw that
Ruby-throat himself was breakfasting
on her roses, without even waiting
for an invitation.

"I heard that you wished
to visit the Flower Market
with me," he said, dipping
his needle-like tongue into
the heart of each rose, while
he never for a second stopped
the hum-m-m-m, that his wings
made ; "and I thought it would
be polite, as you are a female, for me to call."

"Yes, thank you, I *do* wish to go there very
much, for there are so many *whys* that I want to
ask you.   But, please who told you about *me?*"

"Hum-m-m-m um, who ?   The message came to
me quite direct ; if I remember rightly, the little
Oak up back on the hill, with whom you were
talking one day, told an Ant who lived near, the
Ant told a yellow Spider who spreads his nets
every night on Miou's lilac bush in the garden,

the Spider chattered about it to his wife, and the
Wind heard him in going by, and told it to a bit of
dandelion down he was carrying; I caught the down
and took it home to line my nest, and *it* told *me!*"

"Do you call that coming direct?" laughed
Tommy-Anne. "I should think that a very
'round Robin Hood's barn' sort of way."

"Oh no; it is quite direct for *us*. When Heart
of Nature's messengers fetch and carry, even if
the message passes through a hundred beaks and
tongues, it never grows either larger or smaller
than when it started; his servants add nothing,
take nothing; simply repeat.

"Thanks, very nice breakfast, delicious roses;
now that I have done, what can I do for you?"
said Ruby-throat.

"Take me to the Flower Market first, if you
please, and then tell me all the *whys*," she said,
drawing her wide hat forward so that it shaded
her eyes, and preparing to start.

"We are in the Flower Market *now*."

"In the flower *garden*, yes; but it is the *market*
that I wish to see. The place where the flowers
sell honey and buy the life-dust to fill the lunch
baskets for the little seeds," she explained slowly,
and very politely, thinking that Ruby-throat had
misunderstood.

"We are in the Flower Market now," insisted Ruby-throat, perching in the shade of the honeysuckle. "Wherever there is a tree, or bush, or plant, or a blade of grass in bloom, *there* is the Flower Market. All day long and all through the nights, from the time Peboan leaves until he brings snow again, the buying and selling goes on; yes, and even then messages are carried over snowy fields to the brave Witch Hazel."

"I thought," said Tommy-Anne, much crestfallen, "that you knew of some one place where all the different kinds of flowers were collected, something like a flower show, where they are all in one big room."

"Are there any butterflies in a flower show, or moths or bees to carry messages?"

"Oh no! the flowers are only there for people to admire."

"Tommy-Anne, when flowers are at their work filling the lunch baskets, as Heart of Nature bids them, they cannot possibly all live in one place, because they are made to draw their food from different soils, and to suit different conditions; and as they come into bloom at different seasons, different messengers must serve them. How do you think that an April Violet, who loves the shade, the Ox-eyed Daisy of June, and the Rose

P

Mallow, that takes its walk through the marshes in August, could meet in the same Flower Market?

"No; the Flower Market begins in late February or early March, when the monk of the swamps, the Skunk Cabbage, pushes his pointed hood through the gaps in the snow, and it lasts until Witch Hazel receives its messenger, who comes so late that it cannot cast the seed abroad until another spring.

"One week, the Violets call, 'We are ready,' to the little white Anemones — that are so shy that they hang their heads if Gheezis does not smile at them, and they hold the Market; then the trees of forest and river-banks take their turn. Next come the orchards; then the festival moves down among the meadow grasses; next the marsh ferns claim it."

"Trees! grasses! ferns!" said Tommy-Anne, in astonishment; "I never thought that they belonged in the Flower Market."

"And why not? Do you know what a flower is, little House Child?"

"Of course I do," she answered, rather indignantly. "It is a lovely thing that grows on a plant, and it is made of coloured leaves, and some flowers smell very sweet, and some sour, and

some have no smell at all. These pinks and
roses are sweet, but the yellow ones over there
are *very* sour; why is that, dear Ruby-throat?"

But instead of answering her last question,
Ruby-throat said, " You have forgotten the chief
thing : the flower is the bearer of the seed baskets,
and that is its reason for being. Lay one of those
wild roses on your hand and look at it carefully,
beginning with the stem.

" You see that the stem swells to a green cup-
shape, ending in the five little pointed leaves that
wrapped the bud."

" Yes ; and inside that are five pink leaves
fastened on at the bottom ; they are called petals.
I know that, anyway."

" And again, inside of the petals?"

" A lot of little threads in a circle, each with a
puff of yellow powder for a head, and inside the
circle, a bunch of green knobs that come from
the stem-cup."

" That is right. Now of all those parts in
what is called the flower, only two are absolutely
necessary to the growing of the seed : the lunch
basket, holding the seed-germs, waiting for their
food, of which the knob is the handle, and the
balls of golden powder, which is the life-dust, —
the food to nourish the speck of life first until it

becomes a seed, and then a plant.   These powder-puffs are of as many shapes and fashions as the flower itself.   The coloured petals of the flowers may be different in shape, of one piece or many, large or small, or lacking altogether; but if the basket of seed-germs and the life-dust is there, then it is a flower.

"The oak bears acorns, though its flowers are but dingy feathers; the birch's brown tassels from which the golden dust blows are as much its flowers as the sweet rosy clusters on the apple tree."

"But, dear Ruby-throat, if every flower grows its own life-dust, why do they have messengers to carry it to and fro?   Why must they buy and sell?"

"This is the reason, Tommy-Anne.   Even if a flower grows the life-dust, it may not grow it for itself alone, and some plants have blossoms where the seed basket is in one flower and the dust in another; then how could the dust and the basket meet without a special messenger?"

"I can understand that; but this rose has both dust and basket in the same blossom."

"The rose and many others can supply themselves, and usually do so, but oftentimes the dust on a flower may not be ripe when the seed-germ is the hungriest, so Heart of Nature has told the messengers to fetch and carry, that all may be doubly sure."

"Who are the messengers, and how do they work?"

"They are many, and as varied as the flowers they serve,—bees, butterflies, moths, and then always the wind, and for some things the Water Brother, though he is greater as a seed-sower.

"Heart of Nature sends one of these winged transports to the flower whose heart it can best reach, saying, 'Feed from the honey; take your fill of the golden store.' As he eats, the life-dust clings to his tongue or hairy legs or feelers, and he bears it with him to be left on the next flower he visits. So two are fed at once, the insect messenger and the seed. And each blossom has its sign by which its rightful messenger knows it, —colour or perfume,—and not one of them would so far forget himself as to mix the message of buttercups and clover."

"But," persisted Tommy-Anne, "why didn't the first Heart arrange the Plan so as to have the life-dust always tip over into the baskets, without messengers?"

"Because," answered a voice that she knew belonged to her Tree Man, even though she could not see him, "nothing is made for itself alone. The bee is for the flower, the flower for the bee. Dependence is the strength of my garden. Do you remember the password, Tommy-Anne?"

"Yes," she whispered; "it is Brotherhood."

"Tell me about the flower families, please, Ruby-throat, and who is the Queen of the Flower Market?" said Tommy-Anne, who had been silent for so long a time that the fidgety Hummingbird was on the point of flying away. "The Bumble-bee said that the Rose Family is *very* important."

"Here comes Mr. Bumble now; he can tell you himself, for I have an important engagement quite a piece away, but you will usually find me in the garden from sunrise to sunset," said the Hummingbird.

"I have seen you here in the honeysuckle later than that, when it was quite dark."

"Seen me after dark? Never, I assure you; you must mean one of those clumsy prowling Hawk Moths. They always come out, taking the best of everything, when respectable Humming-birds are in bed. Pray do not mix *me* up with butterflies and moths; they are only flying worms, while we come out of nice clean eggs. A little

time, a little food, and presto! we are beautiful
birds.   While those others, do as many tricks and
changes as Wabeno who was juggler to the Red
Brothers.   You should see the
horrible thing that the Hawk
Moth grows from, and you would
never think of mistaking us again."

"Oh, do tell me about all the
tricks, and more about the Hawk
Moth."

Ruby-throat said something about
"asking the Hawk himself," and
was gone with a whirr and a flash.

"How do you do, Tommy-Anne?" said Gitche-ah-mo, the Bumble-bee, his legs dragging
heavily with the weight of the gold dust upon
them.   "When I saw you last, everything smelled
of lilacs, and now the perfume has changed to
grape flowers and roses; but whatever it is, it
means work for some of us bees.   So you wish
to know which is the greatest family in the
Flower Market?   The answer depends greatly
upon whom you ask.   A cow or a sheep would
probably say the Grass, but I think that the birds
and the House People would agree upon the Rose
Family."

"Do birds care for roses?"

"Not much for roses, perhaps, but they are devoted to cherries and strawberries."

"What have they to do with roses?"

"A great deal, Tommy-Anne; for they belong to the Rose Family."

"I don't understand about this one single bit; *why* do they belong to the Rose Family? what makes a plant family?"

"There are great divisions that come first, — the plants with flowers, and the plants with only rusty seed spots on their leaves, like the ferns. Then those whose sap veins run up and down the leaves, and those where the veins run across like spider webbing. Then plants who thrust up a single finger when they leave the seed, like the grass and corn, and those that reach out two, like the bean, for by these signs and many others the plant world is divided into races, and after that the families are made from the plants whose habits follow some one of the many designs."

"Then if a plant is not like any other, it has to be a family by itself?"

"Yes, Tommy-Anne, and the House People have given these orders and families long Latin names; they are not easy to remember at first, yet they all have a meaning, and you must learn them before you can know how plants that look wholly unlike at the first glance may be first cousins."

Meanwhile Mr. Ah-mo had disappeared in a great white foxglove bell, but he soon backed out again, smothered in gold dust.

" Please tell me the names of other flowers that belong to the Rose Family, and which one of them is the ruler."

" The Rose herself is the Queen," said Gitche-ah-mo, in his rich bass voice, " and her brothers, the Plum and the Pear, help her. There is a great deal to be done in this household, and some members of it are busy in the Flower Market from Cherry time until the Moon of Falling Leaves. The best garden fruits belong to this family, — the cherry, and his wild mates, the apple, quince, pear, plum, strawberry, raspberry, blackberry, — and beside these fruits, the thorns and other flowering shrubs."

" *I* think it ought to be called the *jam* family," cried Tommy-Anne, clapping her hands at the idea. " I don't wonder that you roses hold your heads so high," said she, to the big bush nearest to her. " I'm very much obliged to you, I'm sure, Madam Rose, for having so many lovely children, and cousins, and brothers, and nephews, and nieces ; why, we could have a whole garden and orchard without going out of your family but that would be what people call 'very exclusive,' which father says is a greedy, bad habit." And she made a courtesy to the bush and gave each open rose a light kiss in its heart, throwing a handful more to the other bushes.

"Pooh!" said a great scarlet Poppy, tossing its fiery head; "you might take some notice of *me*, for one of my family grows a juice that will put you to sleep in a minute."

"I don't care one bit for that," answered Tommy-Anne. "Going to sleep is easy enough; if the juice would wake me up in the morning as quickly, it would be of much more use to me."

"You lovely Butterfly!" she exclaimed, as a yellow beauty, barred and edged with black, its lower wings ending in long points, fluttered by, passing spray after spray of blossoms in search for something that he did not find. "Will you have some roses for breakfast? Ruby-throat said they were delicious."

"No, I thank you," he replied; "I am not a messenger for that family. I serve much humbler plants,—many of those that House People call weeds; but if you have any parsley in the garden, I will breakfast with you."

"We have plenty of parsley, but it never grows

old enough to have flowers, because, you see, we are always nipping it off to flavour things."

"I smell some carraway flowers, over there in the herb bed," said the Butterfly; "they are cousins to the parsley, so I will visit them."

"Have you any name?" asked Tommy-Anne.

"Because of my stripes and long wings, I am called Tiger Swallow-tail, and I have many brothers shaped like me, but of differ-ent colours," said he, pois-ing on one of the um-brella-shaped clusters of the carraway flowers and raising his wings until they met above his back, while he sipped a little aromatic honey.

"Why did Ruby-throat say that butterflies and moths are only trick worms with wings, not coming straight from a nice clean egg, as he does?"

"It is true that as *butterflies* we do not come directly from the egg, and at best the longest life among us is but a short year, yet the changes we go through from our birth to our maturity are mysterious and strange. I don't wonder that the Hummingbird thought them Wabeno's tricks, but does he not know that as a magician Wabeno is a bungler compared to Heart of Nature?

" This is our life history briefly told : the females of our family lay their eggs one by one on a leaf. After some days a caterpillar is hatched. It is deep green and wears a sable band and turquoise buttons in black settings. This caterpillar, after feeding greedily upon young willow leaves or sprigs of ash and poplar, lies down to rest in the groove of a leaf, weaving a little silkeu shawl about itself."

"Oh yes ! " cried Tommy-Anne, in delight ; " that is a cocoon. I gathered a great many of those things last summer, but they wizzled away, and nothing ever came out of them."

"No ; this little veiled caterpillar is not the cocoon ; that is why no butterflies came out of yours. After the caterpillar has rested, he moults the shawl, and goes to another leaf and eats again and rests, and he does this until he has rested and moulted four times, all the while growing larger. At last he spins a web and draws a leaf together until it closes around him like a hammock, and in this he makes the bed in which he lies during the two or three weeks that it takes, in summer, for his wings to grow, and finally he gnaws the web away and crawls out a full-feathered butterfly."

"Full-feathered? Do butterflies really have feathers, or is that only a way of speaking?"

"They have feathers. This colour upon my wings is made of feathers as perfect as those the birds wear, but from their fineness you think them only dust."

"Where do you live in winter, Mr. Swallow-tail? I have never seen any of your brothers hereabout, and you look so frail that I should think the frost would wither you, as it does the flowers."

"In our family, two broods are raised every season, and we full-grown butterflies die in the autumn. The worms that have spun the late cocoons live hidden away in them all winter because of the cold, not coming out as butterflies until the spring. But every family, whether of butterflies or moths, has its own habits. Some of us sleep the long winter sleep as butterflies, and die in early summer after laying the eggs, while others fly away in autumn to warmer countries, migrating with the birds."

"Fly away like birds? Which ones are able to do that?"

" There are some of that family over yonder in the field. Come with me, and they shall tell their own story."

At that moment Waddles raced up. He had been trying to help Obi, who was busy cooping two broods of newly hatched chickens; but his company had proved very unwelcome, and he barked and bayed at his mistress, vainly trying to make her see that his intentions toward the chicks were of the kindest, and that he felt very much grieved at the suspicion that Obi cast upon him. So to keep him quiet, Tommy-Anne allowed him to join her, and Swallow-tail led the way to the field.

The grass was tall and uneven, the most conspicuous flowers being pale yellow thistles and quantities of common milkweed. Butterflies were almost as thick as the flowers, — brick-red butterflies, edged and ribbed with black. They were strong of wing, too, taking straight aim and flying direct, not fluttering about in the undecided manner of their kind.

Swallow-tail whispered something, and a bevy left their work and came gracefully toward Tommy-Anne.

" So Ruby-throat has been mocking us," said the foremost, " calling us ' flying worms ' ? He had better not boast, I can tell him, for there is not a beak in all Birdland that dare even so much as *bite* one of us!" And his companions waved their wings in approval.

Tommy-Anne did not speak, but she *looked* as if she thought this statement rather a whoppergrass, and the butterfly continued: —

"Frail as I look, I am named the Monarch, and I can fly hundreds of miles without resting, passing over seas from island to island, like the fleetest-winged bird.[1] Last September, when my black, white, and yellow caterpillar had completed his changes, and I came from the cocoon, I joined my brothers in the great waste fields over the hills by the salt water, where are acres of the milkweeds for which we are the messengers.

"Shaw-shaw, the Swallow, was gathering his flocks at the same time. We circled together over the sands, and travelled southward, casting shadows on the water-ripples as we passed over. Some of us tarried in Florida with the Thrushes,

---

[1] See Guide to Butterflies, H. S. Scudder.

but others passed onward to the islands in the wake of the Swallows. All winter long we toiled for our bread in the Flower Market, but among such flowers that the very sight of them would make our home-staying brothers turn into beetles with envy.

"Then, stopping to give greetings in all the Flower Markets by the way, I returned; and now when the first eggs of the year are laid, my life work will be done."

"Why didn't the birds eat you?" asked Tommy-Anne, incredulously. "You must have met a great many hungry ones in travelling so far."

"Heart of Nature protects us. He has wrapped our bodies in a magic perfume that is hateful to birds." And the Monarch fluttered close to her face for a second.

"Oh, oh!" cried Tommy-Anne, pinching her poor little nose tightly together. "I don't call that a *perfume;* it is a *smell*, and a *very bad one*, too. Thank you, that is *quite* enough; I understand *perfectly* why the birds do not eat you."

"So do I, mistress," said Waddles. "I once caught one of these Monarchs, and, between ourselves, *I* think it ought to be called the Skunk Butterfly!"

But the Monarch overheard, and, taking offence

at Waddles' remark, called his companions, and
prepared for a long flight, saying angrily, " If
this is the way you treat us when I am kind
enough to tell *whys*, we will go away and live on
some one else's milkweed flowers ! "

" Oh, please don't," cried Tommy-Anne. " You
should not be vexed at Waddles ; for your
perfume, though it does not seem nice to *us*,
must be a very *useful* smell to you, just as the
Skunk's is to him ; and I dare say that there
are some things that might think both of these
smells delightful ! "

" You are right, Tommy-Anne," said the Monarch, in a tone of apology ; " a smell may be very
useful and not ornamental, so to speak.

" It is the same with the marsh plant that the
House People call the skunk cabbage. Its rank
odour calls the bee messengers to him, across
some half-thawed swamp as quickly as if it was
as the heliotrope itself." Then the whole flock
of Monarchs began to flutter and rise for their
flight.

" Monarch, Mr. Milkweed Monarch ! " she
called as they scattered, " won't you please tell
me what sort of a worm the Hawk Moth comes
from ? Ruby-throat says that it is a horrible
thing ; but then he seems to dislike this moth."

Q

"I would rather not say anything about it," answered the Monarch. "Ask the Hawk himself; he will be sure to visit the honeysuckles to-night, or else the petunias or lilies, for he carries messages for many deep-throated blossoms."

"I suppose we must wait," said Tommy-Anne to Waddles. "Heart of Nature's things do not seem to like to tell tales about each other. What shall we do now?"

"We might go and see how Obi is managing with the chickens," answered Waddles.

"*We might*, but *we won't*," said his mistress. "I will attend to Obi and the chickens, and you may go and *rest* on the piazza. Mind, sir!"

The bees held high carnival in the garden all the afternoon, — bees of all kinds and descriptions, hive bees, wild bees, carpenters, and bumble bees, all bustling and repeating the flower messages in such loud voices, that if there were any secrets among them, they were pretty well spread abroad. As the sun lowered, one by one disappeared, zigzagging home in different directions.

Waddles had come to grief soon after dinner, by poking his nose into a hornet's nest, and was now in a shady part of the garden, with his bumpy, swollen face buried in the fresh earth, trying to imagine that he had not been foolish.

The birds were having a grand concert, for there were young ones in almost every nest, and hosts of members were trooping to the Robin Club in the cedars. After supper, Tommy-Anne walked up and down by the honeysuckle trellis, waiting for whatever might turn up ; for since she had worn the Magic Spectacles something interesting was all the time happening. The new moon was slipping down the sky in the northwest, and the sight of it reminded her of what the little Oak had said about the Moon Moth and the Land of Nod, where the flowers slept. Then she felt something fly lightly by and touch her hand. She looked again, and there was an exquisite moth, actually resting on her sleeve, its gauzy wings spread flatly, and not fluttering like some of its butterfly kin.

"You wished to go to the Land of Nod, so I have come," said a silvery voice.

"What are you?" whispered Tommy-Anne ; "a moonbeam?"

"Not that, but the next thing to it. I am the Moon Moth," he said, spreading his long-tailed transparent wings, that were of the same shimmering green as a young poppy leaf when the dew lies on it, and touched here and there with bark-brown edges and brilliant eye-spots like the markings on a flower petal. Except for his stout, furry body, he was more graceful than any of the day butterflies.

"How could Ruby-throat ever call a beautiful thing like this, a 'flying worm'?" thought Tommy-Anne; but she only said: "You are very good to come for me, and I shall be delighted to go; but please, is the Land of Nod a long way off? Because in the evening I may only go about the garden and a little way up the hill yonder, and then, only when it is moonlight, and this moon is so young that I think it will soon have to go to bed."

"Tommy-Anne," replied the Moon Moth, "the Land of Nod is both far and near, for it is wherever the Flower Market is held."

"Do the poor flowers never sleep, then?"

"Surely they do. Those who have done their work by day close their lids and fold their hands, sleeping as peacefully as you yourself; but there are other blossoms who only begin their labours as Gheezis disappears, and we are their messengers, we moths, the heavy-bodied flyers of the shady hours and of the night, for it takes the moths' long tongues to reach the honeyed hearts of the deeply tubed night blossoms. See, the white ipomea, that is called the Moon Flower from its blooming time, is already waiting on your arbour for its guests, and the honeysuckle buds are breathing their first best perfume."

"Honeysuckles are open all day long," said Tommy-Anne.

"They stay open in the day, it is true, but their first freshness and sweetness has passed by. That gleams and wafts through the darkness to lead their messengers, the Hawk Moths, to them. Hark! I hear them coming now."

There was a whirring, even louder than the winging of the Hummingbird, and several dusky shapes hovered above the vine, dark and mysterious as bats.

"*Please* keep still one minute, so that I can see you," pleaded Tommy-Anne. "I have heard so much about you from Ruby-throat."

"And nothing good, I'll warrant," said the Hawk Moth, poising for a second on the back of her hand, so that she saw that he was broader than her palm, with wings striped and spotted with gray and black, while a row of orange spots dotted the sides of his hairy body like tiny lamps. In fact, near by he looked fierce and hawk-like enough to deserve his name.

"Ruby-throat does not half like me," he continued, returning to the honeysuckle; "you see, we are honey rivals, visiting many of the same flowers, and as I come out at night when they are opening, I have first choice, and he has to take what is left the next day. But he should not grumble, for he may eat nice green lice, while the law of *my* family forbids eating meat. I suppose he called me a 'flying worm' or something of that sort?"

"I — I believe he did," said Tommy-Anne, reluctantly; "but he didn't tell what *sort* of a worm you come from; he said I must ask you."

"He did, did he? Well; my dear, I must confess that in my first state I am not attractive, or in any way agreeable to the House People. In fact, I come from that extremely disagreeable fat green caterpillar, with white lines on its sides and sting horns on its tail, who raises such a rumpus among the tomato and potato vines."

"That dreadful great beast, as long and thick as one of Obi's fingers, who burns you so if you touch it when you are picking the vegetables, and makes such a nasty mess when you tread on him?"

"The very same. You see I am not so conceited but what I know all my bad points; but as a moth I work with a will and do my best in the Flower Market to make up for my unlovely past."

"Please let me see your beak ; it is very curly and seems longer than Ruby-throat's."

"I have no beak, Tommy-Anne. What you call a beak is my hollow tongue ; that I can curve and bend and thrust into the heart of the slenderest flower tube, leaving the life-dust as I steal the honey."

Then the Hawk darted to the other side of the trellis.

"How do you moths know the way to the flowers when it is quite dark?" asked Tommy-Anne of the Moon Moth, who still rested on her sleeve.

"Heart of Nature has given light, shining colours to these flowers and pungent perfumes to be their signals, according to their needs. Even now, the evening primrose, has unbound its shining yellow wheels, and their fragrance floats afar."

As the moon grew paler, the fireflies began to gleam, and dance about, at first keeping low, and then gradually rising, until they seemed to Tommy-Anne to become confused with the stars.

"What are those little bits of light down in the grass? Are they lame-winged fireflies that cannot rise?" she asked.

" They are the wingless wives of the others, and because they always keep on the ground, House People often call them glow-worms. See! one is crawling under a low-spread spider-web that the dew has covered with its diamonds."

"Dear Moon Moth," said Tommy-Anne, "you said a little while ago that some flowers go to sleep the same as I do; are there any such nearby that you could show me?"

"Yes, all about the garden and meadows the blossoms are nodding and drowsing, each one taking the sleeping position that it prefers. Look behind you at the poppies; their heavy heads are drooping, and their petals closed flatly, and the blue lupins, their neighbours, droop their leaves like half-closed umbrellas."

" And," said Tommy-Anne, in an awestruck tone, " the sweet peas are all drawn together, and the single roses, that were so wide open this morn-ing, are curled up as if they had dreadful cramps. Oh, oh! all these little things in the long border are hanging their heads and gaping as if they were simply *falling over* with sleep, and couldn't stand up another minute; and only see the dew on this dandelion fluff-ball! there is a drop on every single feather!"

" Come up the hill a step or two," said the

Moon Moth, floating on in advance, "and see the red clover and the daisies. The clover leaves are folded and bend over to cover the flowers, and the daisies stack their rays or hang their heads."

"How many lovely smells there are about, and what hundreds of strange sounds!" said Tommy-Anne, sniffing the air in delight. "I am sure I smell peppermint."

"Yes, you are walking through a bed of it now; every time the night wind blows it sends abroad the breath of some wild herb."

"What was that?" cried Tommy-Anne, half alarmed as something overhead moved from branch to branch, half flying and half leaping; "it can't be a Bat."

"It is a Flying Squirrel. He seldom comes out in the daytime, for he likes night silence; this year he lives in the hollow chestnut on the hilltop."

"What made this trail along the grass where the dew is brushed away?"

"That is a rabbit track," answered Waddles, putting his nose to the ground and looking at his mistress slyly; "would you like to know where it goes? I should be happy to find out for you."

"Waddles!" said his mistress, warningly. Then she sighed, and said to the Moon Moth,

"How I do wish I could see the little wood beasts and the night frogs and things all at once ! Do you think I ever can ? "

" I am not sure," said the Moon Moth, hesitating ; " there is only one way that a House Child may see all these creatures of the night woods, and then only if Weeng, the sleep spirit, and Wabeno, the juggler, are willing."

" Do tell me the way, and how I can ask Weeng and Wabeno," asked Tommy-Anne, clasping her hands.

" At the full of the June moon, all the beasts, and frogs, and night birds gather at the moss circle on top of the hill, and hold what we call the *Forest Circus*, and if you are allowed, you will see things there that never happen anywhere else, or at any other time, for distinguished guests are invited from other places, some great beasts coming even from the far-off Adirondack wilderness."

" But where can I find the two spirits, to ask their leave, dear Moon Moth ? "

" On the night of the full moon, go, before it is dark, to the moss circle where you often play with Waddles ; wait there until little Oo-oo comes, and he will tell you what to do. The primroses are growing restless, and the moon is asleep, so good-night, Tommy-Anne."

"Mistress," said Waddles, as they reached the house, "if you can do without me for a little while, I think I should enjoy taking a walk by myself in the Land of Nod, to see if I can 'catch a Weasel asleep.' I have heard that it is a very great thing to do."

"Come home, you silly dog," said Tommy-Anne, holding him by the collar; "isn't being stung nearly blind enough of an adventure for one day? Suppose you should meet a Scent Cat! You would have to be buried up to your neck in the earth for a whole day to make you un-scented; for Obi says that is the only cure for any one that meets a Scent Cat *suddenly!*"

XI

THE FOREST CIRCUS

AFTER Tommy-Anne had spent much time in
studying the almanac, *the* day came, the day before the night of the wonderful June full moon,
when the circus would be held in the wood. She
felt so fidgety that she almost quarrelled with
Obi, and nearly cried before she finished the sew-
ing lesson that she always took with her mother,
at the same time that her father taught Obi.
She begged for her supper at five o'clock, but no

" Are we early enough ? " — p. 239.

one thought anything about that, as she was very fond of being out at the time between daylight and dark, and never strayed far.

An hour later Tommy-Anne walked slowly up to the woods, which were on the home lands and the place where she first met Heart of Nature.

" We must wait in here by the moss circle," she said to Waddles, " until we hear the little Oo-oo calling, and *mind*, you are to be *very* good and not speak to anything unless it speaks to you first. Here he comes now." And the Screech Owl flew to a birch above her head.

" Are we early enough ? " she asked anxiously.

" Early enough for what ? " he answered cautiously.

" To ask Weeng and Wabeno if I may see the Forest Circus."

" Of course you are, — too early, if anything," said Oo-oo, snapping his beak. " The only thing for you to do, is to take your place, and if Weeng and Wabeno *wish* you to see, when the circus comes you will see it ; if they do *not* wish it, why, you will not see anything but what is here now : that is all. However, you may as well come and take your place, because as no House Person ever sees the circus but once, it may amuse you to watch the audience come in.

"No ; you mustn't sit there ; that platform belongs to the band ! "

" Do you have a band at this circus ? "

" Do House People ever have a circus *without* a
band ? "

" No, come to think of it, a band is a *must be* at
the circus, and peanuts too. How do you manage the peanuts ? "

" *We* never have anything half so vulgar, and
we have a much greater variety. In the intermission, the ushers pass around baskets of wild
strawberries, new honey, fresh ants'-eggs, currant
worms, hickory nuts, and shelled corn, so that
every one may eat to his liking."

" What kind of a band do you have? brass
instruments and drums?"

" Not exactly, but it makes as many different
noises as a brass band.

" Dahinda is the leader, and his family are the
bass drummers, swelling up their stomachs and
beating on them for drums ; the Ruffed Grouse
are the kettle-drummers, and they roll a splendid
rat-tat-tat with their wings, in some way of their
own which is a profound secret. The Tree-Frogs
are fifers, and all the Crickets, Grasshoppers, Katydids, and Locusts are fiddlers, using their legs and
wings for instruments. But come, you must find

a place; that crooked log yonder will do nicely, and I can perch behind you and explain everything."

So Tommy-Anne seated herself, leaning comfortably back against a tree.

"Will there be any big beasts here to-night? I know that none live hereabout, but the Moon Moth said that distinguished guests were always invited from a distance."

"So they are *invited*, but very few ever come. It is too conspicuous for them to travel at this season of the year, when there are so many House People in the woods. We have to content ourselves this time with two Wild Cats from our own mountain, for chief beasts, and a Museum Great Auk, for the distinguished bird."

"A Museum Auk! Pray, what is that?"

"A *stuffed* one, of course. He lives in Washington, and was down in the work room the other day being repaired, when the Moon Moth carried the message to him. The Auk said that, though he might be late, he would come if he could hire a bicycle; but he never did fly, even when he was young, and it was more than fifty years since he had even flopped a step."

"Will there be any Wolves here?" asked Tommy-Anne, nervously, as she heard a strange noise, between a bark and a howl.

R

"The Wolves are *never* invited," said Oo-oo. "There has always been a prejudice against them ever since, in the nice little Island over seas, a Wolf ate up Red Riding Hood's grandmother. In fact, the animals dislike Wolves, as much as we birds do the English Sparrows. We invited Mishke-Mokwa, the Black Bear, from the wilderness, but as he never answered the invitation, and as the Hummingbird who carried it did not return, we think that perhaps it never reached him. A bear is a *very* distinguished guest, you know; isn't afraid of anything and even dares say, Boo! to a Wild Cat.

"Here come the Whip-poor-wills. They are the eriers who sit in those trees by the entrance, to tell the hours, and remind the beasts that it will soon be time for the circus to begin. See what an odd way they have of perching up and down the branch, instead of across it as I do. It is a great idea, for they look so like the tree that nothing can see them from above or below, when they keep quite still."

"Whip-poor-will! Whip-poor-will, churk!" they began to call lustily, and ten Gray Rabbits took their places at the sides of the opening, ready to usher in the guests. At the same time Mr. and Mrs. Ko-ko-ko-ho came hurrying up, carrying between them a long roll of white birch bark.

"They are bringing the programme," said Oo-oo, "and they repeat the rules, if necessary, and announce the performers, because they have strong voices. Mahng the Loon was asked to do it, but he goes up North at this season for his health, and does not dare take the risk of coming back."

The Horned Owls hung the roll, which proved to be a sort of banner, between the trees at the entrance. It read thus:—

FOREST CIRCUS

PATRONESSES

MRS. RUFUS LYNX.	MRS. ADJIDAUMO.
MRS. KO-KO-KO-HO.	MRS. ALASKA SABLE.
MRS. RED FOX.	MRS. JACK RABBIT.

I

MUSIC BY THE BAND.

Tune.

The great big drum said, "Bom, bom, bom."
The little fife said, "Wee, wee!"

II

Dance by the Woodcock Brothers.

III

Song and Chorus by the Grasshopper Family.
"Katy did, she didn't, did!"

IV

MUSIC BY BAND.
Tune.
"Jump, froggie, jump!"　(*By request.*)

V

Jumping contest between Spring and Tree frogs.

VI

Race by Chipmunks on Living Bicycles.

VII

Dance of Fireflies and Moon Moths.

VIII

MUSIC BY BAND.
Tune.
"You'd better go home while you can."

RULES

I

NO ONE SHALL KILL OR EAT ANY ONE ELSE ON THE
CIRCUS GROUNDS!

II

ALL DISPUTES SHALL BE SETTLED BY RUFUS LYNX,
THE KING OF WILDCAT MOUNTAIN!

"That programme is written in plain English," said Tommy-Anne, in astonishment, to Oo-oo. "I shouldn't think that the animals could read it."

"Now, on the contrary," answered Oo-oo, "it seems to *me* to be written in plain Owl. You see every one reads it in his own language."

Tommy-Anne had no more time for asking questions. The audience was gathering. A group of small fur-clad animals came in together, and ranged themselves close by Waddles and Tommy-Anne. They seemed to be very tired and warm.

"Mistress!" whispered Waddles, "there is a Skunk sitting next to you!"

"Alaska Sable, if you please, before company," replied the animal mentioned, looking danger. "You call me Skunk, Scent Cat, and other mean names, in summer-time, but when you wear my fur in winter, you call it *Alaska Sable*. Now if you like to say Skunk, say it to your muff, not to me."

"I beg your pardon," said Tommy-Anne. "I really did not know that you and that nice dark fur were the same person. You see, I never came near enough to you before to tell what you really look like. Will you please give me the name of your brown next-door neighbour?"

"His common names are Stoat and White Weasel, but when he is made into cloaks he is called Ermine, and the House People are very proud to wear him."

"Ermine? why, that is white fur with little black tails sewed all over it."

"*Now*, to be sure, he is dusky; but when the snow comes, and he sheds his summer coat, his winter fur comes in soft and white, and his tail is tipped with black."

"How w-o-n-derful!" said Tommy-Anne; "and the other two, who are they?"

"Members of our family. The smallest, with the sharp nose, is the Mink; he always keeps the same name. And the larger one is the Pine Marten; his fur-name is Hudson's Bay Sable! A grand name that, but unlucky; it costs a great many Martens their lives."

"And the fur costs a great many dollars to buy, if that is any comfort to the family," said Tommy-Anne, her eyes rounding with surprise at all she was hearing.

"I wish they would hold this affair in winter," said Mrs. Ermine, sharply, fussing and fanning herself with a large oak leaf. "My wardrobe is out of repair, and I really cannot manage to have a new gown before cold weather."

"You do look shabby," said the Alaska Sable, who had a habit of always agreeing with people in a disagreeable way.

"I'm nothing to the Foxes," snapped Mrs. Ermine, waving her fan toward a family party who were entering. "If I looked like them, *I* should stay at home!"

"Their children have nice gowns and are very well fed," said the Marten, trying to be pleasant. "I should not be surprised if that eldest son made his way in the world."

"Yes, if the way lies through poultry yards," said the Mink, who was a sad chicken-thief himself, and recognized a new rival in Master Fox.

Numbers of birds now began to troop in, — Hawks, Owls, and Herons from the marshes, while half a dozen Ruffed Grouse took their places on the musician's platform.

Mr. and Mrs. Wood Duck followed the Bittern, but wisely did not bring their family; for Foxes are Foxes, rules or no rules, as they knew only too well. Mr. Duck apologized for not bringing any other members of the Duck Family, but he said that all the other kinds had gone to spend the summer by the sea.

Soon a party of Woodchucks arrived, then more Foxes, and a family of Raccoons, then a bevy of

Red and Gray Squirrels, Chipmunks, Weasels, and Rabbits.

Flap, flap, flap! and the air was dark with scores of little brown Bats, who soon tucked themselves away behind leaves, where they hung by their wing hooks, like cloaks.

"There is no more room; why doesn't the circus begin?" asked Tommy-Anne of Oo-oo. "Ah! here come the Moths; I never dreamed that there were so many different kinds."

"The guests of honour are not here," said Oo-oo. But even as he was speaking there was a bustle, and the audience all crouched down in their places, for in stalked Mr. and Mrs. Rufus Lynx, and the ushers trembled so, that they fell up against one another like tumble-down card houses, and could hardly lead the way to the great chestnut opposite the entrance, where a large limb had been reserved for the Wild Cats.

Mr. and Mrs. Lynx gazed about for a moment, giving strange grins by way of greeting, and finally settled down on their branch, looking uncomfortably as if they might spring at any moment.

" Mistress," said Waddles, his teeth chattering, "it would be very bad for me if they should see me. Cats hate dogs. The Miller's cat is

only a mouse to them ; do you mind if I sit
on your feet instead of up here? I have been
very nervous ever since I was sick." And he
slipped down and tried to hide under the edge
of her skirt, which, however, was so short that
it only tickled his ears.

Then there was a great puffing, and rustling,
and Ko-ko-ko-ho announced : —

"His Grace, The Great Auk ! from the Smith-
sonian Institution. His only appearance ! The
laziest bird of his day, who sat still in one place
so long that he lost the use of his wings, and so
all of the family perished. He has ridden the
entire distance from Washington in twelve minutes on the celebrated Ananias bicycle, — the
ONLY WHEEL in the market warranted to be
made of *one solid piece*, and with handle bars
adjusted to armless riders ! Circulars may be
had of the ushers !"

Then His Grace appeared, out of breath and
dusty. He was over two feet high and seemed
to be all body and beak, for his wings and tail
were only big enough for a pigeon. He wore a
dusky, hooded cloak and a white vest, while the
white patch under each eye looked like a pair
of crooked spectacles.

"Water," he gasped, "and a cool stone to sit on."

The Rabbits brought him acorn cups of dew, but they seemed very unsatisfactory to a mouth that could hold a pint. There was a consultation, and then Ko-ko-ko-ho asked politely, "if His Grace could walk down to the river?"

"Not another step! not another inch! I'm so dry that I should crack all over. *You* little know how it feels to be in a museum for years and years; many and many a time I've nearly choked to death from the powder they sprinkle over me to keep the moths away. My! won't they worry if they find I am away on a vacation! I'm worth *hundreds of dollars*, because there are no more of me!"

"That must be the only reason," giggled Waddles, indiscreetly.

"What's that? what's that? Reason enough, *I* think. It should be a most encouraging example to things that are not appreciated by the public, to know, that if they only follow the advice of the hen to her chicks when she sees a hawk, 'Make yourselves scarce!' they will, in time, become priceless. It was not for nothing that I sat still until I lost the use of my wings," said the Auk. "I had this object in view all the time and —"

"What fools these *old Auks* be!" interrupted a piping voice.

" Who said that ? " shouted His Grace.

" I did," continued the merry voice, "though the words partly belong to a sayiug that is much older than you.   I'm a Puk-Wudjie, and the

twenty-fourth great-grandson of Puck-the-First, who was a very big fellow in the Forest Circus that was held over seas at this same time of year.   In fact, he did most wonderful acts; he put a belt around the earth's waist and tied it in a beautiful bow-knot in forty minutes, and there were no bicycles then either! This ancestor of mine was a great friend of a man named Will the Swan, who wrote down the story of that Forest Circus, and that is the way the sayings of my grandfather have been kept."

"Water, water!" gasped His Grace again, feebly, not caring to argue with some one whom he could not even see. Fortunately two Herons, who had disappeared at the first alarm, came flying back from the marsh with half a dozen pitcher plants full of water, and as soon as they were emptied down his great throat, the Auk recovered sufficiently to squat on a flat stone close to Tommy-Anne's log, where he sat gaping and fanning himself with one of his foolish little wings.

"Turn up the lights!" ordered Ko-ko-ko-ho. It was then a soft twilight, a blending of moon and sunlight, but quite dark among the heavy trees. As the Owl spoke, instantly a firefly gleamed from every leaf around the circle and high up in the trees above, while their humbler wives twinkled in the moss. "Don't forget the rules, especially the second one," called Ko-ko-ko-ho.

"I think that this is likely to be a very peaceful circus," said Waddles, peeping out of his retreat.

There was a double row of fireflies in front of the band stand, and as Dahinda raised his baton,

a magnificent roll of drums followed. The fifes replied, and in a second, all the varied sounds of a summer night were going in full force. The tune was very popular, and the musicians received an encore. Then the Crickets twanged their little banjos and played a dance measure, very well known in poultry yards, called —

"Fly high, Rooster! Wing and toe it!"

and the Woodcock Brothers stepped out and made their bow.

First they ran rapidly around the circle in opposite directions, with wings spread and trailing, then stopped short, facing each other, doing a jig step, flapping their wings, and calling "paa-p! paa-p!" every time they changed feet. Next they shot into the air, waltzing about each other until they were quite out of sight, but soon dropping slowly again, singing to the time-beats of their wings.

"Woodcocks really do dance, even when they are not in a circus," said Tommy-Anne, confidentially to Waddles. "Obi saw them in the spring on the edge of the bog woods, and he said they went up ever so high and kept saying the same words every few minutes."

The Katydids next came out to sing. The evening waists of the ladies were trimmed with pale green chiffon, and the large sleeves were of the same material, but according to the custom of their family they wore knickerbockers instead of skirts. They had some difficulty in getting into key and then in keeping there, but the chorus was superb and ended in a burst of sound like escaping steam.

Just then there was a cry of fire ! Several of the ladies' sleeves seemed to be ablaze, but it proved to be a false alarm, merely a firefly who had dropped from his hook and become entangled in the finery.

The band played, —

"Jump, froggie, jump ! There's a snake behind you ! "

while two Tree-Frogs, and two of their brothers from the spring, took their places on the starting-line, ready for the jumping contest. This line was rather movable, as it was formed of small turtles placed side by side ; and as soon as the ushers had arranged them, one or two would move to watch what was going on, and it all had to be done over again.

" This is very tedious," said His Grace, puffing and gasping so that he nearly blew out the lights of the fireflies nearest to him, and wafted Tommy-Anne's hair into her eyes.

"Did your mother never tell you it was impolite to breathe in people's faces ? " she asked.

" I don't remember anything about my mother ; mine was only a Humpty-dumpty nest, you know. I never had any home, and I brought myself up."

"Poor thing! That accounts for his manners," thought Tommy-Anne.

"This is *very* tedious. I wonder why I came," repeated the Auk.

"I don't know, I'm sure," replied Tommy-Anne, seeing that he expected to be answered. "I think that you would look much more suitable in your glass case at the Museum."

Then His Grace was offended again, and turned his back on Tommy-Anne, much to her relief, and the jumping contest proceeded.

By this time the Chipmunks dashed in on their bicycles, and the attention turned to them.

Their machines were the oddest things that Tommy-Anne had ever imagined. The wheels were large toad-stools with little brown ground-snakes for tires; the frames were frogs, who held wish-bones in their mouths for handle bars; the saddles were grasshoppers, whose long legs made fine easy springs; while the chain and other parts were formed by inch-worms holding each other, head and tail.

After riding gracefully twice around the circle and saluting the distinguished guests, the Chipmunks dismounted. Immediately the bicycles unfastened themselves and stood in groups, chatting. Then each rider took his racing colour

from an usher (which consisted of a cap made
of a rose), and set it jauntily on his head.   One
was red, one white,
and one yellow.
The bicycles put
themselves to-
gether, the
snakes drawing
long breaths to
inflate their bod-
ies, and holding
their tails firmly
in their mouths;
the Chipmunks sprang on their
wheels, humping their backs for
business.

The race was a quarter-mile
spurt, in six laps. For two laps they kept
almost together, Red Cap and White being, if
anything, a little in the rear. They all had
considerable difficulty with the handle bars, because the frogs kept forgetting themselves and
turning their heads to look about.

On the fourth lap, Red Cap shot ahead, and
Yellow Cap dropped several yards in the rear,
then White Cap pedalled up only a length behind
the leader, and Yellow Cap was forgotten.

Red Cap had half finished the last lap, when the tire of his front wheel collapsed (the snake, having become tired of holding his breath and his tail at the same time, let go of both), the wheel broke to bits, and the rider turned a summersault, upsetting White Cap, who was so close behind that he could not stop. The several parts of the shattered wheels ran off in different directions, leaving their riders to walk home, while Yellow Cap won the race easily, and received the prize, — a basket of cracked corn prettily decorated with cones.

Refreshments were then served, and every one nibbled and talked.

Suddenly there was an awful growl; no! two growls. The audience grew silent and slipped back to their places; the ushers spilled the refreshments all over the ground, and tried to vanish down imaginary holes.

Horrors! Rufus Lynx was standing on his branch, twitching his sharp ears, lashing his stumpy tail, and snarling —

" A fine way this, to treat distinguished guests. No proper food has been offered to us, and we wish some *immediately*, or we shall help ourselves ! "

Terror was written on every face; the Auk

turned pale, and the birds all began to try their wings, while the small animals gave themselves up for lost.

"Food, food! Bring us food," snarled Rufus again; "at least a Rabbit or a Partridge apiece."

Growls still louder than those of the Wild Cats sounded outside, and even Rufus cowered, for the ground shook, and in trotted a great Black Bear, with worn, dusty fur, and a scrap of chain hanging from a collar that was around his neck.

"Woof-oof!" he snorted, "what's the matter here? Having a row? I'll settle all that for you; calm down, you two little kittens!" And he stood erect and shook his paw tauntingly at the Wild Cats.

"I suppose you all wonder why I didn't answer the invitation to dance at this circus, and why I am so late. The truth is, my dear brothers, my fame as a good dancer has led me into a great scrape; the House People heard of my accomplishment, and last spring, when I was lean and hungry, they caught me in a trap and have been leading me about by a chain ever since, to be a peep-show for children; they call me Ursa Major, the tamest Black Bear in America!

"Am I tame? NO! Shall I ever be tame? N—O! I am simply temporarily obliging them, for reasons of my own. I should be caught if I tried to escape now, but when we travel northward again, in the Moon of Falling Leaves, *I* shall *disappear*, some night, and be at home before the snow falls to betray my track." And he gave a wink so wide that Waddles thought he was being swallowed.

"I have come here now to dance for you, while my employers, who left me chained for the night in the Miller's barn, are down in the village buying bitter, brown foam-water with the money I earn for them.

"By the way, do I smell honey? I love honeycomb, when it is served *without the bees!*"

The ushers instantly went to a hollow tree, that was used as a refrigerator, and dragged out a fine honeycomb on a grape leaf.

Ursa devoured this in great glee, daubing a goodly share on his paws, and asked for more. When he had eaten four combs, wax and all, he said that he was ready to dance, as he dared not wait until the end of the programme.

"Perhaps this charming House Child will give me the honour of a waltz," he said, going to Tommy-Anne, and holding out his paw with a very polite bow, but with a very treacherous expression in his eyes, which as much as said:

" Perhaps this charming House Child will give me the honour of a waltz." — p. 260

"Even if it *is* against the law to kill or eat anything on the premises, I will give her one bear's hug, and *then* she never will tell any one of my plan of escape."

"Mistress!" barked Waddles, frantically.

The lights went out. There was a sound of scurrying feet; Tommy-Anne trembled so that she did not dare look up.

"Mistress, you sat still so long that I thought you must be asleep; and you know what Obi says happens to people who go to sleep in the woods; they have a chill, and next day their bones grow rusty and creak : his did, you know."

"Asleep? Nonsense, Waddles; you know we have both been to the *Forest Circus*, and the Bear made a rumpus and stopped it before the programme was half over. Isn't that true, little Oo-oo?" But the Owl was not there!

A whistle blew from the direction of the house, and Tommy-Anne answered it as she arose slowly and walked down the hill. Could Waddles be right? She did feel a little stiff. On the grass lay a couple of moths quite dead. One was a pink and buff Pine Moth, and the other one of her friends, the Moon Moth.

"I wonder if they were hurt in the crowd at the circus," she said to herself. "No, I think a bird has bitten one ; anyway, I can keep them for my own." And she laid them carefully in the crown of her hat, which she held like a basket. When she reached the garden she found her father waiting for her at the gate.

"It is almost eight o'clock, little daughter. Why! you look half asleep already. So you have been moth-hunting? Did you see Puck or the fairies anywhere about in the moonlight?" he asked jokingly. "Your mother thinks it time that her owlet came in-doors."

"I haven't seen any fairies, father dear; but Puck's *very*, VERY great-grandson was there, and he said : 'What fools these old Auks be!' to His Grace, which wasn't polite, to say the least, — only Waddles says he didn't!"

<h1 style="text-align:center">XII</h1>

KO-KO-KO-HO AND THE BAD ONE

A SEPTEMBER wind storm was scolding and shaking everything, and Tommy-Anne looked out of the study window with a very rueful face, for she was afraid that the birds and growing things would be all blown away at once.

The great elm tree swayed to and fro, knocking on the roof every time that it bent, as if it was trying to summon help. The empty Oriole's nest bobbed into sight as the drying leaves were torn down, and then the wind shook the windows and whistled shrilly in the chimney, driving the smoke from the hickory logs into the room.

"I never felt such a blast before, even when I was the tallest tree in the grove," said the Forestick, trying hard to keep near the back log and not roll out on the hearth.

"How long ago were you a tree?" asked Tommy-Anne.

"Two years back, if I remember rightly, and I had stood in the same place full eighty years, storing up sunshine that I might give it back in fire warmth."

"O-o-u-hf!" coughed the solemn brass-headed andirons; "Oughf-ker-chew, ker-che-w-w! It takes a good deal to make *us* sneeze, but we can't stand this, and so early in the season too! We must look up our winter flannels; I do hope those moth-millers have let them alone. Ou-ghf! That housemaid has set us so far back in the chimney that the draught blows down on our shoulders, and she has forgotten to give us even so much as a pocket handkerchief."

"You haven't any pocket," laughed Tommy-Anne, coming from the window; and kneeling on the bearskin rug, she began blowing the smoke up chimney again with the heavy brass bellows, crying: "Stop, Mr. Wind! you are very impolite, you are choking me, and the bear's eyes are full of ashes.

"What sort of a wind are you, to make it so cold to-day, when yesterday it was like summer? Are you Kabibonokka, bringing winter? If you are, please wait a few days until Obi has finished taking up mother's plants. You should have sent us word that you were coming so early."

" I am not Kabibonokka, but the messenger to say that he is soon coming. I am Keewaydin," cried the voice in the chimney, " the clean wind of the northwest, the peacemaker who stands in the half seasons between the other winds.

" The Red Brothers called me the ' home wind,' and to-day I come to brush earth and sky free from summer heaviness. Suggema, the Mosquito, disappears at my voice, and O-o-chug, the house-fly, beats against the window in despair. Yesterday Shawondasee was here, driving his white horses, the sleek round summer-day clouds, and for all the warning that *he* gave, it might still be the Moon of Strawberries, so I step in and cry, ' Kabibonokka has left his ice fortress, and though he travels slowly, beware ! He is lighting the great winter lamps in the northern sky that flare and stretch up to greet the pole star. These lights are the only bonfires that the White Bear ever sees.

" ' Get you home before his coming, plant blood, and all ye tender ones of Birdland, and you, House People, light your hearth-fires, that you may give defiance to Kabibonokka and his heatless fires of the north ! ' "

" Please, Keewaydin, what are clouds made of, and have they names ? and do *all* the winds drive them for horses? And what is the cold fire that Kabibonokka lights? I thought *hot* fire was a *must be.*"

"Clouds are the tangled skeins of vapour that the sun draws from the air and the watercourses of the earth, which float about until we, the Brotherhood of Winds, collect and shape them.

" Four kinds of clouds are horses for the wind's chariots, and we all drive them equally. The soft white clouds of summer days belong chiefly to Shawondasee and Mudjekeewis; the thin long clouds that stretch like bars above the sun's rise and setting, as if a gate was spread across the heavens, are shared among us all, as are the angry black clouds of many shapes, that we beat and harry until they yield their moisture back to earth. If the summer wind is the driver of these last, then the House People say, ' It rains ! ' But if winter wind holds the whip, they say, ' It snows ! '

" The fourth clouds are those that roof the sky with crystal whiteness, lapping over each other like scales upon a fish, these are Kabibonokka's steeds. They are born of mists driven so high through upper cold, that their water-drops have turned to ice crystals, and thus locked, they fleck the sky dome like frost-work on the window-panes."

" Oh, I know another *why !* " exclaimed Tommy-Anne. " Those high frost clouds that look like fish scales are what Obi calls a 'mackerel sky,' and says that it means cold weather somewhere, and so it does.   But the cold fire — please tell me about that."

" When the leaves have all fallen, and no birds are heard at night, except the Owl Brotherhood, I will send Kabibonokka to your window, and he shall tell you that story.   You will know him, because he will not come until after the brush beacons have burned on the hills."

" What *are* the brush beacons ?" asked Tommy-Anne, eagerly; but Keewaydin had already whirled out of the chimney, a blaze of sunshine shot across the room, and a pebble struck the window pane.

" Obi must wish to tell me something," said she, jumping from the bearskin, patting its head as she did so.   " Yes, he is outside, making signs.   What is it, Obi ? " she said, opening the window far enough to stick out her head.   " Have you caught any more of the bad rats who ate the chickens ? "

" No rats since yesterday, but there is an awful big Horned Owl sitting up in the Miller's old barn by the woods, and I thought you'd like to see it. I can't go up again now, because I must finish with these geraniums."

"Good! I'll go at once." And she banged down the window, and called Waddles, who had been asleep in the scrap basket as usual.

"What if it should be Ko-ko-ko-ho?" she said to herself. "He might tell me about the cannibal birds, and take me to see the Bad One!

"Waddlekins, do you feel real nice and brave this morning?"

Waddles looked several question marks before he made up his mind to answer, "Yes, if it is not about snakes."

"It may be about *a* snake, and it may be not."

"Then, mistress, if it is a *may be*, and only *one* snake, I think I will come half-way, while I think about the other half!"

When Tommy-Anne and Waddles arrived at the tumbledown barn, it seemed so dark inside that for a moment they could not see anything.

"This is very strange," she said; "I wonder how the Owl got in; some one has closed up the broken window that used to be on the side nearest the woods."

"Yes, they have; and I wish you would take the boards down," quavered a voice from the rafters.

"Ko-ko-ko-ho, is that you ?   How did you come in here ?   You know that you aren't a bit of a Barn Owl."

"I am perfectly aware of that fact, Tommy-Anne, and if I ever get *out*, I will never be caught again in such a trap. The reason why I am here is this. I was very sleepy last night, for the Bad One has been sick for several days, and I have had hard work to find anything that he cares to eat, and so I did not begin to hunt for myself until nearly morning. I thought that one of the Miller's pigeons would make a nice breakfast, and I waited until it should be light enough for them to come out.

"The Miller saw me before I had caught a thing, and I was obliged to dodge in here, and Obi and the Miller's boy found my hiding-place and boarded up the window until this afternoon, when they have time to catch me."

"I don't think that you deserve to escape," said Tommy-Anne. "The idea of your trying to catch those pretty pigeons. I don't think that it would be right for me to help you."

"The Miller raises these pigeons for *House People* to eat; where is the difference?"

"A great deal of difference, *I* think. If *you* eat a pigeon, it is eating one of your own people, but for us to eat them is the same as if *you* ate a grasshopper."

"Do House People *never* eat House People?"

"Never!" cried she, fiercely; "that is — at — least — *real* House People never do. There are some wild people that live in islands in the hot countries who do eat each other sometimes, I believe, but they are called cannibals, and all the real House People try to stop this awful habit."

"What do they do about it?"

"There are different ways. Some countries try killing them, and others do all they can to teach them better ways."

"I think," said Ko-ko-ko-ho, "that the best way would be to kill all the old ones, and then teach the young ones. There is a saying in the family of the House Fourfoot that applies to this."

"You can't teach an old dog new tricks!" said Waddles, promptly. "But Mistress will not believe me."

"I only said that you were not an *old dog*," replied his mistress. "But according to what *you* say, Ko-ko-ko-ho, you should be *killed*, for you certainly are an *old Owl!*"

Ko-ko-ko-ho nearly fell from his perch in surprise at the turn things had taken, but quickly righted himself again, and said with an air at once solemn and decided: "The House Child forgets that in good society, the *present company* is *always excepted!*"

"I'll tell you what I will do," said Tommy-Anne. "I'll let you out, if you will take me to see the Bad One, and tell him not to come near me!"

"That is a fair offer. I will accept it with pleasure, and the quicker I get out, the quicker we can start. I will go first. Follow carefully, for the way is rough."

Tommy-Anne had quite a struggle to get the boards down from the opening, but she finally succeeded, and Ko-ko-ko-ho flapped out.

"I think," said Waddles, "that as the Bad One is ill, I will go all the way with you."

It was a long, hard scramble up the rocky hill.

T

Old decaying stumps made the ground treacherous, and the pine needles slipped away from
under-foot, and the shade of the hemlocks and
oaks was black and gloomy.

"This is a very pokey place," said Waddles,
"and I wish for once that Obi was with us."

"I don't like it very much myself," said
Tommy-Anne; "but if the Bad One is very ill,
he may soon die, and as he is the *very last*, I must
see him; but I don't mean to go much further.
I wonder if that is the ledge."

A sort of low cliff, of layers of coarse granite,
made a wall not far in front of them. There
were small trees growing from the crevices here
and there, and flat places worn smooth like steps.
On the top of this ledge were great broken trees.
All was in shadow except the face of the rock,
which was in bright sunlight.

"Sit down where you are," said a voice, and
Tommy-Anne saw, in the flickering light, that
Mrs. Ko-ko-ko-ho was perching close by her on
a stump; so she seated herself on a log, and
Waddles drew himself up beside her, feeling
rather anxious.

"You have been so kind in letting out my husband, that I will sit here to be sure that the Bad
One does not come too near," said Mrs. Ko-ko-

ko-ho, pleasantly. "See! he lies at the door of his home; he has not been out further to-day."

Tommy-Anne looked intently to where Ko-ko-ko-ho was speaking to some object on the ground, and she suddenly felt very grateful that the snake that she saw was both old and sick. There lay five feet of mottled, dusky ugliness, with a threatening head that curved as it joined the body, — eyes that had a strange, slantwise expression, while between them and each nostril was a deep pit-mark, like a sunken scar. The other end of this weird thing was finished by a row of brown, bony-looking knuckles that grated as the tail moved, making a sound like a broom when it sweeps a sanded floor.

Then the body coiled, and the head raised threateningly. "Why do you come to mock at me? what do you want?" he hissed.

"I came because I wished to see you, and to know why you are so poisonous and have those pit-marks on your face. Lac has no such scars, nor the Hog-nosed one, either."

Crotalus lowered his head, swinging it from side to side like a pendulum, as if he felt himself at bay and longed for escape, — tried to dart forward, then, feeling his own weakness, crouched on his coils.

" The answers to your questions are written in the tragic history of our race. None of us may tell it, except the last one of his tribe, and he only when he is about to die. Truly you have chosen the right time for coming.

" Mind, I do not tell the story now because I like you, but because I must. For I hate everything; all are against me, and I am against every one. I am the Spirit of Evil, who exists in different forms to prove the greater strength of goodness. Heart of Nature has set the brand upon me in the death-fang and pit-mark, that all may know me. All the woodland creatures will laugh when I am dead, but even then, Fear will keep them from rending me apart.

" Two families are involved in this legend, that of the Copperheaded One and my own. Once in far back ages when this earth was young, and there were no people, either tent or house dwellers yet living, these two serpent families were as brothers, in all the cliffs and ledges. Both had their lairs, their passages among the rockways and swamp grasses. Food was so plentiful, and life so easy that, the spark of evil in them being greater than the good, they had to make a cause for discontent, and so began to argue as to which family was the greater.

" Much talking led to blows, and one unhappy day the heads of the two families met alone, and sprung on each other, hissing, rolling, twisting, bitiug, until at last the Copperheaded One fastened his teeth in my ancestor's face, and he, with one last spring, shook himself free and gave back the bite with interest, killing his brother !

" Then he slunk back to his hole, trembling for the punishment that must follow. Thus it came. Heart of Nature set the brand on both the families, saying, 'After this you shall be shunned of beasts, and war shall be between you and those the earth knows not yet. Poison shall lie in your fangs, and scar-marks of this quarrel shall ever pit your faces. The Copperheaded One shall strike unheard, but you, Crotalus, murderer ! shall sound a death rattle, telling of your sin wherever you go, and you shall become the symbol of evil.'

" This all came true, and our ill fame fell even on our harmless cousins, far removed, who have no fatal fangs ; for no evil deed injures one alone. And when Heart of Man, the last of all created things, appeared, he scorned us also, and when a snake crawls forth, the cry is ever, Kill ! kill ! The Red Brothers used the poison from our fangs to tip their arrows with death, then wrapped these arrows in our skins and sent them forth as messengers of war ; so death and hate followed us, and we are waning, and I, even I, the last of my own tribe, who once was powerful in this ledge, am dying because of the hatred and the treachery in me. To-day Ko-ko-ko-ho did not bring me food to my liking, and I, not knowing that he had been imprisoned, and being angry, struck at him. But being feeble, I slipped and dashed my fangs against a stone, rending them. This was my death blow, and now I go in from the light of day to pay the penalty. Quickly I must go, for no beast shall see the last Bad One die ! " And Crotalus crawled painfully into the crevice above the rock, which was polished by fifty years of his comings and goings.

The Owls were silent, and so was Tommy-Anne, while Waddles shivered.

" You look as if you would like to go home by a nice open road," said Mrs. Ko-ko-ko-ho, with great sympathy ; " I will show you a short way."

Tommy-Anne gladly followed her, and before they were clear of the woods, Ko-ko-ko-ho flapped after them, calling in a voice that echoed afar off :

" Crotalus, the Rattlesnake, is dead ! The last Bad One has left our ledge ! "

Quick as a flash, little beasts began to appear

from stumps, ground holes, and rock crevices, all running helter skelter and making joyful sounds. Tommy-Anne counted half the animals of the Forest Circus in the space of two minutes. The ground creatures were the happiest, and though it was day, when they were usually napping, the Weasel, Mink, and the Scent Cat — excuse me, Alaska Sable — danced out into the road hand in hand, followed by a great string of Rabbits turning summersaults.

"Now, Waddles," said Tommy-Anne, drawing a sigh of relief, "there is nothing more to poison us in all these woods ; isn't it jolly ? "

XIII

THE BRUSH BEACONS

THE apples were stored away and the nuts all gathered. The Adjidaumo and Chipmunk families had filled their pantries to overflowing; in fact, they had several storehouses each.

Tommy-Anne rejoiced in a bushel of hickory nuts, half as many chestnuts, and several pecks of hazel nuts, which lay heaped on the attic floor, and near these piles hung a store of strange things that people never eat, which were hoarded for her out-door brethren, — acorns, spruce-cones, ears of corn, bundles of oats and rye, and a basket of various kinds of dried berries and seed-pods.

In these days Tommy-Anne's fingers were stained all colours, from a bruised greenish yellow to dirty black, and as to her nails, one might have supposed that they were in deep mourning for the death of Summer ; but it was only because she had been trying to persuade butternuts and black walnuts to come out of their shells before their due season.

There had been exciting times while the nutting lasted, and many games of hide-and-seek with the Squirrel Brotherhood. Now it was November, and Tchin was the only gleaner about the oak trees, while the Flower Market was quite sold out, a few pansies and chrysanthemums in the garden, and some yellow threads of witch hazel in the low woods, being its only tenants.

Tommy-Anne and Waddles had been sitting before the study fire listening to stories of goblins and fairies, and many of the quaint legends of Hallow Eve, and, as usual, Tommy-Anne did not wish to go to bed, when there came from the fire logs a soft purring voice that said : " The Brotherhood of Beasts keeps watch to-night, and we, the Fire Spirits, will be there also. Look on the hills for the brush beacons ! "

" How can I ? " she whispered, " for I can't possibly go out all alone."

"Beg of the winds that come every night to your window; ask them to bring you the news. As for the beacons, you could see them plainly even if you did not wear the Magic Spectacles."

Then Tommy-Anne changed her mind about going to bed, or rather to her bedroom, and soon a bundle consisting of a little girl, with her night-gown over all her clothes, rolled from head to foot in an eider-down quilt, might have been seen pressing her nose against the window-pane and listening intently for some expected sound.

"How soft and warm you feel," she said, patting the quilt.

"Yes, we flatter ourselves that we know how to keep out cold."

"We? Is a quilt a *we?* I always thought that such things were *its.*"

"The outside may possibly be an *it*, but the inside is certainly a *we;* for we are the best part of the Eider Duck Family, and our name is Eider Down."

"You are little feathers, then, aren't you?"

"Feathers, but most superior feathers, — soft as silk, springy as wire, and light as dandelion seed, with no sharp backbones to prick and scratch. The lack of backbone is the stamp of aristocracy in the Eider Down Family, and if any sharp feather appears in a comforter, it is an impostor, and not of us."

" Do you grow to be made into quilts ? "

" Quilts are inventions that the House People made when they first saw *us*. In the north country, where Peboan is king and Waw-be-ko-ko and Wabasso princes, the birds wear very warm clothing, and especially those who never travel far southward at any season. Now, of all these, no bird carries a finer feather bed than the Eider Duck, and when in June he makes a nest of sticks, gray moss, and grasses, he lines it deep and soft with his home-grown down.

"In time the House People saw these nests. 'Ah, ha!' they said, 'we will make nests for ourselves like these, only gay silks and other stuffs shall hold the feathers, instead of sticks and straws.'

" Then what did the greedy House People do? They stole the linings of these nests and returned each season, stealing again, and shooting the nest-builders, until at last a pound of gold will scarcely buy a pound of us!

" Hush! voices are calling! Our friends, the winds who used to talk to us in our rocky Labrador home, are speaking. Listen!"

" The Winds of Night! The Winds of Night!

Who has work for us?" cried the voices, whispering about every crack in the casement, and trying the chimney flues to see if there was any soot to blow down, shaking the shutters to try if perchance a hinge was missing, then veering off again to test the strength of the brown leaves that still clung to the oaks and beeches.

Tommy-Anne looked out the window, and, far and near, about the farms on the open hills, bonfires blazed; some high and straight, others low and straggling, as if they followed old stone fences. "The brush beacons!" she cried.

"The Winds of Night! The Winds of Night! Who has work for us?" called the voices once more. "We bring one ship to port, we leave another upon a rocky bed, we drive the frost before us, and we tear the leaves away. We sweep the heavens clear that the stars may greet each other; we drive the clouds until they crash and drench the earth with rain, and we also bring fair weather, for we are both kind and cruel!"

"If you feel like being kind to me," said Tommy-Anne, "I wish you would tell me some *whys* and then bring me a few messages from the Beast Brotherhood yonder. If you please, which wind are you?"

"I am Wabun, the East Wind," said a voice;

"my home is in Wabun Annung, the Morning Star; my brethren are called elsewhere, and I must keep watch until Kabibonokka lights his fire and comes himself."

" When will that be, Wabun?"

"To-night, when the quarter-old moon has set."

" Did you see Wenonah, before you left the Morning Star? Wenonah, that Robin Thrush and the Bluebirds loved so much?"

" Ah, yes, I have seen her often."

" Tell me about her. Is she very happy? and does she have a garden and plenty of birds to sing to her?"

" Hush!" said Wabun. "Happy she is, but further my lips are sealed; for if the House People that live in *this* earth knew what lies beyond, they would not be content to wait and live their lives out. The Plan says that they must not know, save that *It Is!* But your other questions and your messages, what are they? I will fetch and carry for you willingly."

" What are the brush beacons for, Wabun?"

" They serve a double purpose, Tommy-Anne. At·this season, the House People, who plant the earth with seeds, that they may yield food for themselves and the beasts that serve, have gathered in their crops. Then they rake the refuse, stubble, brush, and all the rubbish that gathers, into great heaps that must be burned before another sowing time. They choose some quiet night like this, to light these fires, before Kabibonokka and Peboan come to scatter and to bury."

"You are blowing to-night; do you call it still?"

"I am here, but I do not fret and spread gustiness. I only whisper, that Heart of Nature may not miss the wind's voice altogether. When the Brotherhood of Beasts sees these fires, they come out from their holes and runs and hide-ways, and talk of winter plans, divide the hunting rights, and tell the happenings of the year, while they keep watch about the fires for warning of Kabibonokka's coming. Then the roll is called, to see if any of the brothers have disappeared since the last brush beacons burned, and then they go their several ways; for among the nearby beasts, some hunt at night, some in the day, some sleep the winter sleep, and some work for their food all through Peboan's reign."

"What is the 'winter sleep'? The hoary Woodchuck told me that he sleeps the 'winter sleep'; is it different from the sleep of night? And if the beasts sleep all winter, how can they live so long without food?"

"The winter sleep is somewhat different, although the beginning of it is the same as the sleep of night. Down in his deep wood hole the Woodchuck is already sleeping it. When his time came, at the first cold weather, he went in, far from the light and cold, and curled his well-fed body round and round, nose to tail, and began to draw deep breaths, at first like the usual sleep. Then, as the days went by, the breath comes fainter and fainter yet, until a House Person could not tell that the life-spark was still there."

"Why is that?" interrupted Tommy-Anne.

"Because a fire that burns slowly lasts a long time with little fuel. The breath is the life-fire of the beast, and the slower it burns, the longer can the body last without food-fuel."

"Yes, yes! I understand that!" cried Tommy-Anne, in glee. "How very *unreally* truly things must seem to people who do not know Heart of Nature's reasons for everything! I wish that I could hear what the little beasts are talking about. Dear Wabun, will you listen, if they have no objection, and then tell me what they say?"

"I can do better than that, for I will bridge space between you and them, and you shall hear for yourself. But when the moon sets, and Kabibonokka's fires are lighted, I must speed away to greet him. Look steadily at the long fire-line in the meadow, between here and the woods, and wait!"

Very soon Tommy-Anne could see the shadowy shapes of animals creeping about into the fire-light. There was some confusion, as if they were grouping themselves in a particular way, and she heard a sharp voice say: —

"If all the brethren are here, I will call the roll."

"All are here that can come," replied Ko-ko-ko-ho.

Tommy-Anne had not seen him since the day that the Bad One died, and she had been afraid that some one had shot him, for Obi and the Miller's boy both said that he still had the pigeon habit.

Mr. Red Fox called the roll from memory, as a Fox never writes anything down, lest it might be used against him some fine day. This is *one* of the reasons why he is called sly.

Though he knew, without asking, that he was present himself, he called his own name, that all the formalities might be complied with.

"Red Fox? Here!"

" Rufus Lynx?" No Wild Cats responded, and after a few minutes Ko-ko-ko-ho answered that Rufus did not dare come, for his wife had stolen a turkey from the Miller last night, and that the spies are out on the mountains, watching the whole family.

" So that is where Obi and the Miller's boy went, a little before dark; and Obi wouldn't tell me where they were going, because, I suppose, he was afraid that I should have asked to go," said Tommy-Anne. " And so I should, and father would have said, ' No, little daughter, it is too far, and too late '; but Aunt Prue would have sniffed, and said, ' Highly improper ! ' "

" Pine Marten ? " continued the Fox.

" Here! in this tree. I don't like to come down on the ground, for fear of wetting my feet with dew."

" Weasel ? "

" Here ! in the old stone fence."

" Ermine ? "

" Here ! but I must soon hurry home to make arrangements for changing my coat."

" Mink ? "

An indistinct choking whisper followed.

" Speak louder," said Mr. Fox ; but the choking continued.

U

“Fan him!” shouted the Scent Cat; “he is dying!”

“Hold him up by the tail and shake him,” called the Raccoon. “He has a spiny-perch fast in his throat; I saw him bringing it up from the river half a second ago.”

After a deal of shouting and struggling, the fish was pulled out, and the Mink answered, “Present!” in a very feeble voice.

“Why don’t you *chew* your food like a respectable long-toothed animal, instead of bolting it like a Kingfisher?” said the Fox. “This is the third time this year that you have nearly choked yourself. In the spring it was with a duck’s breastbone, in the summer it was Dahinda’s fat grandmother, that stuck in your throat.”

“I know, I know,” pleaded the Mink; “but then you see, what with the people who want my fur and those who try to trap me in their chicken yards, I am always on the jump.” And he rubbed his pointed rat-like nose and shivered down to the tip of his brown tail. “To bear the name of ‘chicken thief,’ as I do, keeps me in a hurry all the time, and I seldom can afford myself the luxury of a good chew.”

“Alaska Sable?”

“You need not ask him; we *know* that *he* is

here," cried all the beasts in chorus, coughing and choking.

"How is this?" asked the Fox, putting his handkerchief to his face ; "has any one been hunting you ! "

"I must apologize," said the Scent Cat; "it was a mistake. A stone from the fence rolled off on me as I came over, and not seeing what it was, and thinking that it might be the House Fourfoot, I gave him a hint that he had best not come any further."

"Listen to that, Waddles," said Tommy-Anne. " You see what might happen to you if you chase strange animals, and remember how terribly crampy it would be to be buried up to your neck ! "

Waddles, being asleep under the bed-valance,

did not answer ; in fact he was snoring away in a little whimpering fashion of his own.

" Raccoon ? "

" Here ! " answered this little cousin of the Black Bear, hurrying up with a half-stripped corn-cob in his mouth. " It was well that the beacons burned to-night, for we go to sleep to-morrow."

" Do you sleep all winter like the Wood-chucks ? " asked Tommy-Anne.

" Not *all* winter, but the greater part of it. Our family do not like soft snow, so we go to our tree holes early and put our children comfortably to bed.   We wait for the late winter sleet storms to crust the snow with ice, so that we can walk without sinking, and then we come out."

" When are your children born ?   Aren't they big enough to take care of themselves yet ? "

" They were born iu May, but we keep them with us until they are a year old, when they set up housekeeping for themselves."

" Why do I never see you about in the woods ? Are you getting scarce, like the Auk ? "

" We are few now, compared to what we used to be.   My grandmother remembers when every hollow tree between the mill woods and Wild Cat Mountain held a Coon family ; but the reason why you have not seen us is, that we are night hunters, like Dusky Wing and the Skunk and Flying Squirrel."

" Do all the other animals hunt in the day ? "

" Very few of them hunt in the brightest light, they like the twilight best, the hours after sunset and before sunrise."

" There must be no more talking and answering questions until the roll is called," snarled Mr. Fox. "What if the fires should go out before I have ended?

" Star-nosed Mole ? "

" Here! under your left hind foot."

" Shrew-Mole ? "

" Here! under Jack Rabbit." (Jack immediately moved, as if the idea of any one tunnelling beneath him made him nervous.)

" Flying Squirrel ? "

" Here ! " And a wild grapevine that hung over a tall cedar several rods away trembled, and the speaker made a splendid flying leap to a birch tree above Mr. Fox's head. Then the gray acrobat spread his loose skin flaps that stretch along his sides from paw to paw, serving as wings, and sailed away again, landing in a pine, where he had some high words with the Marten, for it takes little provocation to warm the Marten's temper.

" Gray Squirrel ? "

" Objects to going out at night," said Ko-ko-ko-ho.

" Chipmunk ? "

" The same," replied the Owl.

" Jack Rabbit ? "

" Here! always hereabouts, winter and summer, unless it is necessary for my safety that I should be somewhere else."

" That is all, I believe," said the Fox ; " for we decided long ago that rats and mice should not belong to the Brotherhood."

" You have forgotten me," said the little brown Bat. " But I don't blame you, for I am the last and the least, and all the rest of my family have hung themselves up for the winter in attics and lofts."

" The next business in order," said Mr. Fox, " is the division of the hunting, the hearing of complaints, and neighbourhood reports."

" I should like to recommend one thing to our family," said the Weasel ; " that is, that we should stop chicken-killing for a time, and devote all of our attention to rats. Then the House People will be pleased and see that we can do good as well as harm (besides, these rats eat a great many eggs and young chickens, and we of the Weasel family have to bear the blame of it without having enjoyed the chickens)."

" A capital idea," said Reddy Fox, thinking to himself, " There will be all the more poultry left for me ! "

" I," said the Scent Cat, " would like permission to range over Brother Coon's grounds while he is asleep, and I wish that some of the little beasts who travel all winter would bring me word concerning the streams and ponds, telling me which are frozen and which open, for I cannot live long without water, and sometimes in winter water is the most costly thing we poor Scent Cats can buy. When we have to track and retrack the snow to find an open spring, House People follow our trails, and without even as much as knocking at the door, dig us out of our homes."

" Has any one a report to make concerning new neighbours? "

" I have," said the Mink. " The House People who are living at the place between the hill woods and the mill road have built a fine new poultry house. One half is full of fat ducks, and the other half of laying hens. There will be plenty of chickens there next spring. Also these people are lately from the city and may not know who to suspect ; if some of those chickens disappear, they *may* think that it is a habit of young chickens to die and bury themselves."

"Ha, ha!" laughed Reddy Fox; "*very* good. I've met such people. There were some up at Farmer Hazel's last year. They mistook Brother Scent Cat for a house kitten; thought the county drain was a spring and drank out of it; bought skunk cabbage roots from a berry woman, for Easter lily bulbs; and made posies of poison sumach. But that family never came back; country air didn't agree with them!"

"How is it, though, Brother Mink, that if your family are going to take up rat-catching, you should be interested in the new poultry house?" said Reddy, suddenly.

"We thought that *you* might like to follow the matter up," said the Mink, humbly, winking at the Weasel with the eye the Fox could not see.

"This chicken house will not do you one bit of good," said Ko-ko-ko-ho, decidedly. "*These* House People know a thing or two, and what they don't know already, they are learning. The Butcher's boy has worked up there all summer!"

A chorus of Ohs! and Ahs! arose, which told Tommy-Anne better than any words how well Obi must know the tricks and ways of the Beast Brotherhood.

" This chicken house," continued Ko-ko-ko-ho, "has a stone foundation, plastered with the mud that people use to stick stones together, and in the mud is mixed the sharp cutting water that they call glass! Fine wire, stronger than hickory wands, covers the house on every side, and the door opens, not with a string latch, but with a spring that is turned by a smooth knob like an egg."

" Of course, Obi told them how to build it," said Reddy.

" No, he didn't," said Tommy-Anne, proudly. " Father planned it with what he calls common sense, and there is lots more of it at our house, as you will find, if you try to steal our chickens; and then there's Waddles besides! "

" How foolish we are to talk about these things when a House Child is listening! " said Reddy.

" We can't help it," said Ko-ko-ko-ho. " Heart of Nature has given her the Magic Spectacles, so that she can see and hear, whether we wish it or not."

" I could open that door for you," said the Raccoon, obligingly. " I have paws like hands, and I can turn handles and uncork bottles and all that. My eldest brother used to open the door of the Miller's dairy and take the cork out of the jug of maple syrup and drink all he wanted, and helped himself to other goodies."

"Yes," said Ko-ko-ko-ho, "and for that reason the Miller is now wearing your brother's fur for a cap! That Coon went once too often, stuck his head into a jar of apple butter, and couldn't draw it out again. It seems to me that you are talking through your ears, Brother Raccoon!"

"There are too many House People, and too few of the Beast Brotherhood, for us to take risks," said the Ermine, wisely.

"Especially when you can get any one else to take them for you," said Reddy. "But look! the moon has set, and Kabibonokka's light is flaming in the north. To your holes, brothers! To your homes! Good sleeping, brothers, and to the rest good eating!" And Reddy looked wickedly at Jack Rabbit, who leaped away and bolted into the first hole he came to, which unfortunately proved to belong to a Scent Cat, who gave him a bite, by way of rebuke for his intrusion, saying,

" Considering the circumstances, I will let you go, but another time it will be ' good eating ' for me ! "

Tommy-Anne looked toward the north. The sky was glowing with a wonderful greenish-white light, through which long pink streaks shot upward. These colours rayed and changed, one minute melting together, the next separating until they looked like heated metal bars.

" The northern fire is lit," whispered Wabun, shaking the window gently, "and I go on my wanderings. But I will return, Tommy-Anne, and then I will sing you songs of my playfellow the Sea, and tell you how he counts the gray sands where the Plovers' eggs lie, and the Sand-pipers dance."

The brush beacons had burned out, the trees shook and complained to each other that it was growing colder. There was a whistle in the key-hole and another in the chimney.

" Is that you, Kabibonokka? " said Tommy-Anne, and a vigorous, hearty voice answered, " Yes ! "

" Please, please tell me about your cold fire that I see blazing up there. Is it made of brush, or coal, or log wood? And is Peboan coming soon with Waw-be-ko-ko, the Snow Owl? "

"Peboan comes not until another moon. I am
making all ready. After him, at the first deep
snow, Waw-be-ko-ko follows. As to the cold
fire, Tommy-Anne, it is built of neither coal or
wood; it is the electric vapour that we winds
gather in our journeyings.

"In summer this mysterious force shoots
abroad, under the name of lightning. Later on,
I drive and hustle it to my home at the north
pole, where none lives but I, to be my firelight.
There I kindle it, and as it plays across the northern sky, all know it for a sign of winter, and
through the cold months it rays and pales according to the fuel I can glean. Even now Peboan
fills his pipe with it, and warms his fingers at its
chilly blaze."

"Not in bed, little Owl," said a voice from the
doorway. "Ah! I see, you are looking at the
northern lights. I am glad, for they are so beautiful that I had come to waken you. Your night-
gown on over your clothes; and you have not
been in bed yet?"

"What do *you* call this fire, father dear?" said
Tommy-Anne, ignoring her guilty appearance.

"It is called the *Aurora Borealis*, which means
the northern or winter sunrise."

"Is it a cold fire?"

"Yes, it is cold; it is the form that the electric fluid takes when it is near the poles, little Owl."

"The same sort of stuff that makes lightning and the electric lights in the city?"

"Much the same; but we cannot tell exactly." "How quickly she understands," thought her father.

After he had gone, Tommy-Anne went properly to bed, and lay awake for some time watching the light through the window and thinking, and this is what she thought. "There must be a great deal of it, miles and miles. I wonder if up in the northland they ever try to catch electricity and make it push trolley cars. They would if it came down here." And then she laughed at the idea. "Why, there is nobody to go anywhere up there and nowhere to go, and as the north pole hasn't been found, it isn't anywhere, to begin with."

Then she fell asleep and dreamed of an electric car racing down the side of an iceberg, with a Polar Bear in a sealskin coat and cap for a motor-man, while a lot of Snow Owls were the passengers, carrying their skates in embroidered red bags, such as her mother was making for her.

XIV

THE SNOW OWL'S CHRISTMAS PARTY

TOMMY-ANNE thought the "Moon of Snow-Shoes" a very deceitful name for November, as there was no snow, not even so much as a flurry: but instead, the winds played a hundred pranks and sang snatches of all their tunes, and the weather danced to the music and brought March gusts, May softness, that swelled the buds dangerously, and bits of coppery August haze, as if the Old Year had shaken its scrap-bag over the earth, before beginning housekeeping anew.

Finally December and Peboan arrived together,

as Kabibonokka had promised, and the week before Christmas the snow followed, light and powdery at first, then growing heavier and heavier, until as far abroad and upward as Tommy-Anne could see, there was nothing but a maze of flakes, falling, falling, falling, until her eyes blinked and closed in confusion. But where was the Snow Owl? Where was Waw-be-ko-ko, who was to follow Peboan? Surely winter was there, for the little ponds were ice-locked, and frost ferns grew nightly on the window-panes.

Would the snow be too deep for Obi to go to the mountain for the Christmas tree? So many *whys* flew through Tommy-Anne's brain, and she kept opening the windows so often to see if she could find the answers to them, that, of course, the damp snow clung to her hair and shoulders, and she had a dreadful chill.

"How did you manage to catch such a bad cold?" said Aunt Prue, as she bustled in with some of the well-known bottles of medicine.

"I? Indeed, I didn't do any such thing," protested Tommy-Anne; "I only opened the window, and *it* reached in and caught *me!*"

Now, to Tommy-Anne a cold usually meant being tucked into bed beside a cosy wood fire, having something particularly soothing to eat, and mother near to read a delightful story aloud ; but now the entire household seemed to be upset in some way. Her mother was not well, and her father had taken his writing up to her room, and Aunt Prue, forgetting to tell her how careless she had been, pushed Tommy-Anne's little white iron bed into the study, leaving her to sit up or lie down as she pleased. Even Waddles grew suddenly independent, and trotted off through the snow in spite of his mistress' remonstrances. Surely the world must be coming to an end, thought Tommy-Anne.

After two or three days the young lady felt much better, though she had to stay in the study for fear of draughts. This she did not mind, however, for she could see Obi coming down the hill dragging the precious Christmas tree through the snow, and whistling like mad, and of course he had to come in and help place it in the corner of the study and then put the candles and other fixings on the highest branches, as her father was very busy; so Tommy-Anne soon felt quite cheerful again.

"You ought to hurry up and get well and come out," said Obi, in one of the pauses, sitting on the step-ladder while Tommy-Anne untangled the strings of pop-corn that would curl themselves provokingly. "There's a lot of strange birds come since yesterday, all the kinds from up north; storm blew them down, I guess, and this morning I saw a mighty big white Owl catching mice down in the meadow."

"The Snow Owl! Has he really come? Oh, how I wish I could see him and ask him to come up here!"

"Ask him up here? He'd be so likely to come," laughed Obi, thinking that her cold must have affected Tommy-Anne's head. "Now that all the high things are up and you can reach the other branches, I think I'll go and see if I can't shoot that Owl for you; he'd be a beauty stuffed."

" Oh don't, Obi, don't kill him! Think how sorry his wife might be, that is — at least not until after Christmas. It must be horrid to be killed so near to it, you know." And then Tommy-Anne stopped, knowing that she was twisting herself up and talking what must seem nonsense to Obi.

" Mistress," said Waddles, " I think you are carrying things too far.   Don't you remember that Obi, who doesn't wear the Magic Spectacles, can't possibly know that you expect that Owl to come to your Christmas tree ? "

" Of course he doesn't, Waddlekins dear, and I can't ever explain the reasons either. Never mind; we must coax Aunt Prue to bring all my berries and corn and grasses down from the attic, and we will put them around the room for decorations, and then the birds can help themselves when they come to the tree."

" Obi," called Tommy-Anne, as he was going out the door, " could you possibly catch me half-a-dozen fat mice some time to-morrow ? "

" Yes, to be sure I can; we catch a trapful every night in the barn. I suppose you are going to boil them down for tallow, the same as aunt does.

She always makes mouse tallow every winter; it's just boss for chapped hands."

Tommy-Anne smiled. Was she going to make mouse tallow? She thought *not;* but what she intended doing with the mice was a profound secret.

That same afternoon, a little before dusk, as she stood by the window looking at the light from the lantern that shone through the cow-shed window, where the milking was going on, a white shape flapped up to the window, and perched on the sill, quite startling her.

"Open the window," it said; "I want to speak to you."

"I mustn't," she replied; "I have a snuffle cold."

"Then I must do it myself," said Waw-be-ko-ko, for it was he, as he came through the sash.

"You dear Snow Owl!" said Tommy-Anne, holding out her arms as if she would like to hug him. "I was *so* afraid that I should not see you; and way back in the spring I promised the little Spruce, you know, that I would ask you to my Christmas tree."

"No, I didn't know anything about the tree, and I came very near not hearing about the invitation at all," said Waw-be-ko-ko. "You see the little Spruce was snowed under when I came, and it could not find any one to take the message to me until this afternoon. Then a Rabbit came nibbling by, and the tree told him. I saw the Rabbit in the meadow, but he was so afraid that I should eat him that he would not come near enough for me to hear distinctly what he said. All I could make out was something about 'Tommy-Anne' so I came up to see what you wanted."

"Why did the Rabbit think that you might eat him? Do you eat such things?"

"I *have* done so, but not often, for Rabbits are a great deal of trouble to *carve*. I prefer mice, nice juicy mice; they are so much easier to eat. But when are you going to have the grand Christmas tree? I see a tree over in the corner, but it is not hung with twinkling stars, like the one I saw down in the white house in the village."

"Mine will have stars on it, too, when it is lit to-morrow night. What time can you come? And don't forget to bring some of your friends with you, so that we can have a *real* party; not one of Aunt Prue's 'two is enough' affairs."

"I will come at this same time to-morrow night. I am a day Owl, and my friends would not care to be out late in this cold season; they might not be able to find their way back to their roosts. Excuse me," said he, lurching down to the hearth and snapping up a luckless mouse, who had ventured too far from his hole. " It is always well to have an eye to business ! Comfortable room this, nice fire ! Bless me ! if I stayed here long, I should fall asleep. Good-bye until to-morrow, Tommy-Anne, and don't forget to have some comfortable seats for my friends." And he disappeared through the window.

"Seats for birds ! I wonder what will be best. Now I have it," thought Tommy-Anne ; " the clothes-rack in my room is the very thing, — the one with the wooden pegs ! " And immediately she began bumping it along until it reached the corner opposite the Christmas tree, where it stood, looking rather like a leafless tree itself.

The day before Christmas, Tommy-Anne could hardly keep still. She saw Obi and the Miller's children coasting down the long hill back of the barn, while Waddles raced beside them, barking frantically ; there were troops of strange birds, with bent beaks, picking the seed from the spruce cones in the trees near the house, and there was a great deal of running to and fro about the house, knocks on the side door, and many whisperings.

" They must be bringing in presents," she said vaguely. Then a strange sound came from up stairs, not exactly a mew and not a bark; something more like a whine, the cry of a young animal. Could it be? Was she to have a new dog for Christmas?

She would have liked to have half-a-dozen dogs, but she felt very sure that she would never love any as well as she did Waddles, and then too he might be jealous. No; on second thoughts, she did not care for another dog.

Soon her father came into the study and asked her if she would like to go up stairs and see a very particular present that had arrived very early in the morning. Of course she would.

"Is it for me, or for you, or mother?" she asked; "and am I to guess three guesses before I see it?"

"It is for all of us," her father answered; "and you would never guess what it is, if I gave you a dozen chances."

"Is it an *it* or a *we*? Is it any kind of an animal?" persisted Tommy-Anne.

"Yes, little daughter; it is a 'we,' and it is a little animal with a soul!"

Soon before dusk Tommy-Anne hurried back to the study and begged her Aunt Prue, who was passing the door, to light the tree candles for her.

Aunt Prue thought it was taking a double risk of fire to light them twice, as Obi and the Miller's children were not coming for their gifts until eight o'clock, but she finally consented, after setting a pail of water nearby, in case of accident.

Tommy-Anne waited anxiously until her aunt had left the room, and then hastened to the window. There was a serious expression on her face, and she seemed to have grown taller since morning.

A sigh came from the chimney, and a voice that seemed to come from the logs said, "What is the matter, Tommy-Anne? You are thinking about something. Are you not pleased with your Christmas gifts?"

"My dear Tree Man, are you here? I was *wishing* and *wishing* to see you."

"That is why I came, Tommy-Anne."

"But, dear Heart of Nature," she said, almost sobbing, "I'm not Tommy-Anne any longer. I've broken in half, and *Tommy* is *up stairs*, and *I'm down here!* You see I have a little brother, who came before light, and as I didn't expect him, I had no Christmas present ready for him, so father said that I might give him half of my name, the Tommy-half, and I did. Then I gave him half of Waddles too, — the tail half, because I thought it would wag and amuse him. And so I'm not Tommy-Anne any longer, but Di-ana.

"I always thought Di-ana was a horrid name, called after that stuffy old idol that belonged to the Ephesians; but father says that there were several Dianas long ago, and that one was a very jolly person, who kept a great many dogs and went hunting in the woods whenever she pleased, and *never* tore her clothes! So now I'm more reconciled to my name, and I'll adopt this hunting-lady to be my fairy godmother."

Then a tap came at the window, and she flew to open it, and in fluttered nearly a dozen birds led by Waw-be-ko-ko, and though they were a little dazed by the light, they did not forget their manners, and bowed to Tommy-Anne with great politeness, as she pointed to the clothes-rack, upon which they immediately perched.

"Very kind and thoughtful of you, I'm sure," said Waw-be-ko-ko; "most charming perch. If you please, I think I will warm my claws a bit by the fire ; they will hardly bend." And he walked solemnly over to the hearth ; but when he saw the glassy eyes of the bear's head on the rug, he gave a squawk and chasséed in the opposite direction.

Tommy-Anne laughed heartily, and Waddles rolled out of the scrap basket, seeming much surprised to find so many birds about.

"Will you tell me the names of your friends, and where they come from?" asked she; "I have never seen any of them about in the summer."

"They are all my wing companions from the north," answered Waw-be-ko-ko, "and their nesting haunts are where the snow, even in summer, lingers on the side of things that Gheezis does not see. They come to you with the snow, and leave again before it has melted from under the fences. Brother Shrike, allow me to present you to my friend the House Child!"

The Shrike was rather embarrassed, for, thinking himself unobserved, he in company with the Tree Sparrow, was taking a dip in Aunt Prue's water pail, and was in a dripping condition wholly out of keeping with an evening party. But he flew to the perch, vainly endeavouring to appear at ease.

"Oh! oh! how funny you look," said Tommy-Anne; "won't you sit on the fender until you are dry? Please tell me why you have such a hook on the end of your beak. You look something like a Hawk."

"Thanks, I *will* go by the fire," said the Shrike, in a shamefaced way.

"That hook is to help me catch my food. I suppose that *you* would call me a cannibal bird, for the House People have named me 'Butcher Bird,' because when I catch more game than I need, I hang some of it up on bushes and thorns, as a butcher hangs his meats. To be sure, I *do* sometimes eat my smaller brothers, but like all the others, the Crows, the Hawks, and Owls, the mice and beetles and harmful insects I destroy, when compared to the birds I eat, are as a mountain to a mole hill."

"Do winter birds sing? Do you ever sing, Mr. Shrike?"

"Indeed he does," said Waw-be-ko-ko, "though not in the winter. In his nesting haunts he warbles like a Thrush, and so do these two also, the brown and white brother, the Snow Bunting, and this mottled Shore Lark, who soars and sings above his Labrador nest like his cousin the English Skylark.

"You would never know them in their summer coats, Tommy-Anne, from seeing them now. Brother Bunting is clear black and white, and the Lark wears two black feathers that make him look like a clerk with a pen over each ear, and he has also a beautiful lilac waistcoat."

"Why, what are you doing here, Chipping Sparrow?" said Tommy-Anne. "I thought you had gone away *long* ago; and you too, Johnny Wren!"

"No, no! it is a case of mistaken identity," they said together. "I," said the smaller of the two, "am the Winter Wren, the smallest bird hereabouts, excepting the Kinglet and Ruby-throat, and I'm spending the winter in your wood pile." "And *I*," said the other, "am the Winter Chippy, or Tree Sparrow."

"You three reddish birds on the top of the perch, what are you called?"

"I'm the Pine Grosbeak," said the largest, with a heavy gray body, washed above with crimson, and a stout bill. "I am so named because I build my nest in the low pines of the cold lands, and when winter freezes me out, I come down here to warm myself, again seek shelter in the evergreens, and feed upon their cones."

"I," said the twisted-billed, brick-red bird,

"am the Crossbill, and come from the same regions, and I also seek my food between the cone-scales. See, Heart of Nature has arranged my bill like a pair of pincers, to wrench the cones apart."

"So, then, *you* are one of the birds that I saw this morning in the spruces. I thought that your jaw was out of joint, and it quite worried me."

"I," said the last of the three, with a crimson cap and a beak sharp as a needle, "am the Jolly Redpoll. I can weather anything in the way of cold. I follow man as far north as he may go, and build my nest but a little above his footsteps, and now I am gleaning my food from the seeds in your waste fields, even though the snow flies about me like diamond dust. May I have some of those seeds from the grasses on the mantel shelf?"

"Certainly," said Tommy-Anne. "Please all help yourselves to anything you wish. See, here are some fat mice for you, Waw-be-ko-ko." And she pointed to a lower branch of the Christmas tree, where some field-mice hung by the tails. "What would Obi say," thought Tommy-Anne, "if he knew that he had been catching mice for an Owl!"

The Snow Owl was delighted with his feast, and a peck came just then at the window, which proved to be the Junco, the gray snow-bird with the white vest, who lives all winter in the honey-suckles. He had forgotten about the party and gone to roost, and waking up had remembered in time to join his friends at supper.

For a while all the beaks were nipping, peck-ing, and snapping together. "I should think that it would disagree with you to swallow furry, bony mice without chewing them," said Tommy-Anne to the Owl.

"So it would if the bones and fur *stayed* swal-lowed, but I soon make them into little balls and spit them up again ! "

"Is that a *really truly?*" asked Tommy-Anne, in astonishment.

"Certainly. Ask Ko-ko-ko-ho ; or, if you look on the ground near our home tree, you will find these balls of fur, gristle, heads and tails, every-where about. Different birds, different habits ; that is all ! "

"This pop-corn is excellent," said the Grosbeak.

"*I* like these little apples," said the Crossbill, dipping his beak into the red-cheeked lady apples, with a relish.

"I should like to stay here and build my nest in the Christmas tree," continued the Grosbeak sociably.

"I wish you would," said Waddles, who had

been very quiet, but was rapidly growing tired of the attention that the birds were receiving. "I like squabs."

"I could make a fine nest in that scrap basket," said the Winter Wren.

"No, you could *not*," snapped Waddles; "that is my nest!"

Suddenly the Snow Owl began to cough and hop about the room, flapping his wings as if in great agony, and did not answer when everybody asked what was the matter.

"He has half swallowed a nice red candle, and he's choking," said Waddles, in glee. "It was a blown out candle; suppose we light it again!"

"No, no!" gasped Waw-be-ko-ko; "let me out quick."

"Never mind; it can't hurt *you*," said Tommy-Anne; "for you can make it into little balls and spit them out whenever you please!" And all the birds laughed and thought it was a good joke on the Owl. As she opened the window to let him out, the other birds followed. "What, must you all go? Yes, I see that it is really dark. Good-night, brother birds, and a merry Christmas!"

Presently Obi and the Miller's children came, and candles blazed again and the Spruce tree dropped its wonderful fruit into their hands, and at last the candles burnt out one by one.

Tommy-Anne looked out at the sky, where

Sirius, the Dog-Star, winked gravely at her. She wondered if Heart of Nature was near, and if he would soon come to take away the Magic Spectacles that he had lent her to wear until Christmas Eve. The fire flickered cheerfully, and the winds whispered outside.

"I am here," said the Voice, but this time it came from the Christmas tree.

"Have you come for the spectacles, dear Tree Man?" asked Tommy-Anne, anxiously. "It is so dark that I can't see you, and this is the time, — Christmas Eve. Do you know about Christmas Eve, dear Heart of Nature?"

"Do I know? Yes, little House Child; this is the anniversary of the night when the Three Hearts met and understood one another, Heart of God, Heart of Nature, and Heart of Man;

the Christ Child, the cattle, the shepherds, in the manger at Bethlehem, and at that meeting the password *Brotherhood* was born ! "

Again the winds called and wrung strange music from the leafless branches. The dry snow scurried and settled on the window ledges, where Jack Frost was perching, clad in an invisible cloak, while he traced upon the panes outlines of the forest ferns and greenery that his touch had withered.

The fire crackled and blazed, and Tommy-Anne sat in silence ; at last she whispered softly, "Yes, I understand," and then added with a sigh, "But the Magic Spectacles — I shall not wear them to-morrow. Please tell me of what they are made?"

" You have used them well, Diana, and so you may keep them as my Christmas gift, and by and by you will share them with the brother, when instead of calling you Tommy-Anne, people will say Tommy and Anne. As to these spectacles, the glasses are made of TRUTH, but the settings are fashioned of a strange and precious metal that House People, for lack of a better word, call IMAGINATION ! "

" Mistress," said Waddles, " before I go to bed, I'm going up stairs to see the other fellow who owns my back legs. I think we shall be chums ! "

Y

"The Winds of Night! the Winds of Night! Who has work for us?" called the voices outside the window; but as the fire flashed again, Sirius gazed into an empty room, and Tommy-Anne kept the anniversary of the Three Hearts by a little cradle.

THE END